The Woman In the Sky

ROBERT ISENBERG

AIRMAIL MEDIA

Airmail Media
160 Westminster Street, 2nd Floor
Providence, RI 02903

Printed in the United States of America

For Leo.

CONTENTS

1   The Woman in the Sky   1

2   First Letter   55

3   The Palace of Wayward Dreams   60

4   Second Letter   129

5   The Tercentennial Swordsman   139

"Nothing in life is to be feared,
it is only to be understood.
Now is the time to understand more,
so that we may fear less."

– Marie Curie

The Woman In the Sky

November, 1912

STEP BY STEP, Elizabeth descended the staircase into frigid darkness. Wax dripped down the candle that lit her way. The flame quivered before her, threatening to go out.

Elizabeth could sense the smallness of herself—forearms like twigs, gangly legs, her ever-blinking eyes. Deep within the black cellar, she felt brittle and exposed, a waif swaddled in woolen layers.

Go back, she thought. *You don't belong here. You're out of your depth. This is not the life you want.*

Yet she took another step, and another, plunging further into the abyss. When Elizabeth reached the bottom, she found an earthen floor, and the firm ground gave her small relief. She drifted through the vacuum, aimless, until her candle shed light on a table.

The wood was unfinished and crudely nailed together. A flaxen cloth was spread across its surface. As Elizabeth hovered closer, objects entered the pool of light. Unmarked beakers stood in a row, their tops capped with interconnected tubes. Thermometers lay side by side, and handwritten notes, penned in a microscopic scrawl, covered reams of scattered pages. Strange liquids settled at the bottoms of jars. A Bunsen burner rested in the middle, next to a coiled hose. The scene looked like any chemistry bench at school. It all felt strangely familiar—until she saw the hypodermic needles.

There were five in all, fanned out along the table's edge. The needles were tiny, but the syringes had the girth of full-grown carrots. Elizabeth bent over to inspect them, but when she took a step, her toe struck something hard. She lowered the candle and saw them—two metal canisters, standing upright, next to a rough-hewn table leg.

Elizabeth brushed cobwebs away from one canister and examined the label pasted to its surface. The paper was old and faded, but she could just make out the printed words. She crouched there for a moment, watching her breath diffuse in the dim light.

COMPRESSED HELIUM.

Suddenly, Elizabeth straightened. Her eyes popped. She squeezed her lips between her fingers.

That's it, she thought. *It all makes sense.*

Her heart pounded. Her breaths came hard and fast. Excitement surged through her like a geyser. She staggered backward, toward the staircase.

That's the answer, she thought. *But could it be? Is it really possible?*

She heard a creak. The boards above her moaned. A pair of booted feet stomped across the floor. She looked up, toward the cracked-open cellar door.

A voice called down: "Elizabeth, someone's here!"

Elizabeth's throat tightened. She looked to the table. She saw the notes, the chemistry set, the needles. She yearned to bag them all and take them with her. This was what she needed. This was why she'd come. If she left empty-handed, she would have nothing.

"*Elizabeth!*" rasped the voice. "*We have to go!*"

But Elizabeth didn't move. Her mind reeled. How had she gotten here? Only a week ago, she had been an ordinary twenty-one-year-old, jaded and alone, dragging herself from class to class. Now she stood in a cavernous room, deep underground, trembling with cold and fear. She was risking her life for a man she hardly knew, and she had no idea why. Her vision spotted. She felt herself gag.

Elizabeth bolted for the staircase.

The door slammed shut.

The candle blew out.

❖

"Now I want to show you something *really* interesting," said Dr. Colin O'Malley, as he pushed a skeleton across the floor. The skeleton was suspended from a metal frame, and its platform was outfitted with wheels so that Dr. O'Malley could roll it into the middle of the classroom. He adjusted his spectacles and said, "Now then, what do you think?"

The students all leaned into their wooden desks, eager for a better view. The skeleton was human, all right—but there was something *wrong* with it. Many of the ribs had fused together, forming a gray breastplate. The cervical spine was too thick, as if the neck had melted into the shoulders. Indeed, the vertebrae showed little distinction; each segment blended into the others.

But most shocking of all was the skull—it bulged on one side, as if the sphenoid bone had blown a bubble.

"Was… was it…" one student stammered.

"Go on," said Dr. O'Malley.

"Was it a fire?"

"Ah, a very good idea," Dr. O'Malley said. "But not correct." The other students tittered, but the professor raised his hands. "Now, now, it's a fine guess. But despite appearances, bone does not liquefy. A fire would have turned this specimen to ash."

"Some kind of tumor?" asked another. "In his brain, I mean?"

"Another splendid theory," affirmed Dr. O'Malley. "Yet another illusion, I'm afraid. It *seems* like a tumor might distend the skull, like so. I know many a physician who would agree with you. But that's not what happened here. Any other guesses?"

Dr. O'Malley lowered his eyebrows. He stood on tiptoes, as if trying to spy a distant point. The students recoiled at this gesture; they swiveled their heads backward, to identify whatever their professor was trying to see. Beyond the rows of heads—the well-cut hair, the white collars of lab coats, the stacks of notebooks and scribbling fountain pens—appeared the small face of a girl.

"*Miss Crowne*," said Dr. O'Malley. "Any bright ideas?"

The students all craned their necks toward Elizabeth Crowne. Everyone knew who she was, of course—she was the only girl in the room. But she was conspicuous even so: Her reddish cheeks looked like dabs of watercolor on her pale face. Her skin contrasted sharply with her navy blue dress. Her dark hair formed a subtle wave beneath a thick band, which was embroidered in silver patterns. That metallic thread was the only decorative thing about her; otherwise her vestments were plain, devoid of ornament.

The way she ground her pencil repetitively into her paper, it was clear that Miss Crowne was not writing notes. She was doodling.

Thirty pairs of eyes were now trained on her. Yet the girl was nonplussed. Her pencil stopped and she set it on the desk. She raised her brown irises toward Dr. O'Malley, crossed her arms in front of her, and said, "I don't know…"

She paused just long enough for smiles to form. Anyone in the room could feel the cresting wave of amusement. But then Miss Crowne resumed.

"…*exactly*. But if I had to make a bet, I'd say it's M.O.P."

The tension lifted, and the students traded glances. *M.O.P.?* read their startled eyes. *What in blazes is that?*

Dr. O'Malley's smile was steady. "Would you care to elaborate, Miss Crowne?"

"It's just a guess," she murmured.

"I dare say your peers are not as versed in acronyms," said Dr. O'Malley in his singsong cadence. "For their benefit, perhaps you could explain."

Miss Crowne swallowed hard, then wove her fingers around her pencil. The implement quavered like a dragonfly's wings.

"I believe it stands for *myositis ossificans progressiva*," she said, then cleared her throat. "Very rare, I've heard. The muscle tissue ossifies. Essentially—your muscles turn to bone. Parts of your skeleton enlarge, until it crushes your inner organs. In the end, the patient dies of suffocation." She huffed, lay the pencil down, and crossed her arms again. "But I don't know for sure."

"That's… *repulsive!*" one young man proclaimed. He shook his head incredulously. "Enlarging bones? Crushing the organs? It sounds like a dime-store novel!"

Dr. O'Malley rested an elbow against his lectern. He frowned, then scratched the tip of his nose. "It does at that," he said. "It is a gruesome theory. And it sounds too strange to be true. I trust no one here has ever seen what Miss Crowne has described?"

Learn the Art of Medicine

At Saint Luke's Medical Academy

In the quietude of New England's Berkshires, men are learning the Art of Medicine. Beyond books and rote memorization, our Mentors use hands-on techniques and true examples. To master the Physician's hallowed craft, we believe in the **power of experience**. If Hippocrates were alive today, he'd recommend St. Luke's.

1 Sheffield Road, Quentin County, MA

The students nodded their agreement, and the young man grimaced. "So it must be something else."

"Not at all," Dr. O'Malley countered. He shot a knowing look across the room. "And let this be a lesson—in science, uncanny doesn't mean untrue. Strange as it sounds, this poor fellow had flesh that turned to bone. It's very rare. There is no cure. He suffered terribly, to be sure. But on the bright side, Miss Crowne, your prognosis is exactly right."

❖

If there was one thing in the world Elizabeth relished, it was the conjoined circles she saw through a pair of binoculars. She loved aiming those twin lenses at a distant tree. As she adjusted the focus, the blurs sharpened—into branches, shriveled leaves, and finally, the stark outline of a raven. The black bird stood still, jerked its head, and blinked its round eyes. Then it leapt from its perch and flapped away.

Elizabeth let her binoculars dangle as she trudged across the wet leaves. She exhaled silvery breath into rays of sun, and she balled her fingers inside her wool mittens. She didn't expect to spot much avian this afternoon. The skies were bare and silent, except for the faint honking of geese, as their V-shaped flocks migrated across the faded clouds.

When she reached the creek, Elizabeth saw movement through the trees, and she rolled her eyes at the sight of Abner Cohen.

Abner's hands were stuffed into the pockets of his checkered coat. His eyes were aimed at the ground ahead of him. His furry *ushanka* hat bobbed comically as he moved. It was only when he reached the small footbridge that he looked up and spotted Elizabeth.

"Oh!" he exclaimed. "There you are!"

"Here I am," Elizabeth replied. "And where were you?"

"Practice ran late." He shrugged. "Sorry."

The creek gurgled beneath them as they stood on the bridge, and they leaned over the railing to watch the dark water trickle between the rocks.

"Did you see anything?" he asked.

"A raven. Not much else."

Abner nodded vacantly. "I think you really impressed that new professor. That O'Malley fellow."

Elizabeth's lip twitched, but otherwise she betrayed no interest in this remark. Then she grinned at Abner. She stabbed a mittened finger into his gut and said, "You look like a walrus."

"Well, it's *cold* out."

"Lord knows how you survived New York winters."

"It's chillier up here," Abner averred, snuffling. "And anyway, I work up a sweat on the court. It makes everything feel so much colder. Couldn't we just go inside?"

"Do as you like," Elizabeth said, hugging her binoculars and heading down the trail. "As I recall, *you* wanted to join *me*."

There was a part of Elizabeth that loved to taunt Abner. He huffed and rocked on his heels, but soon he started after her, just as she expected. Elizabeth knew she shouldn't take such pleasure in his discomfort. After all, he was her only friend.

Elizabeth had spent three years at Saint Luke's Medical Academy, and the semesters had crawled. She barely remembered the remedial classes of her first term. Her copy of *Gray's Anatomy* was dogeared and ripped, and every paragraph was scrawled over with notes. The tiny college was one of those old Jesuit schools, sequestered in the Berkshires, swallowed in foothills and forest, miles from the nearest town. Out here, in the gray New England wilderness, isolation made her gloomy. She avoided the packs of students in the quad. Still, they watched her from afar, murmuring among themselves, and she could only pretend not to notice. Most days, she lost herself among the library's stacks, or she locked herself in her special dormitory—until the coast was clear, and she could sneak away, toward the open grounds.

Abner had clumsily wandered into her life. He was a year younger, but accelerated, and they'd shared a dozen classes. He sat near her when he could, but never *too* near. Elizabeth treated him with the same affection as a stray puppy. Every moment he wasn't practicing with the academy's basketball team, Abner invented new reasons to spend time with her. Charmed by his awkward attentions, Elizabeth had finally asked him to go birding. The invitation was absurd; Abner had grown up among crowded Brooklyn tenements, and he clearly didn't like to spend time outdoors. But he'd agreed, without hesitation—amusing Elizabeth to no end.

As she strolled down the dark soil, Elizabeth's eyes cut through the colorless landscape, surveying the naked canopy for movement. The branches sometimes trembled, stirred by the breezes that seeped between trunks; otherwise, the woods were still as a cemetery. And then, the instant she decided to turn around, she saw the flash of crimson.

Elizabeth jammed the binoculars against her eyes and drew an icy breath. To see a cardinal was common among these hillocks, but this specimen still made her heart race: The bird bore soft red feathers, and its eyes glinted within the black mask of its face. The beak was a blunt orange arrowhead, and it hopped on its branch before freezing in place.

Elizabeth watched the bird, transfixed, until Abner appeared at her side, shivering noticeably as he stared at the ground.

"Take a look," whispered Elizabeth, and she shoved the binoculars into his gloves. Abner took them reluctantly and aimed them at the sky. "Lower," instructed Elizabeth. She touched his hands and guided them down and across, until she felt his arms tense.

"Oh… my goodness!" he said. "Is that a… a robin?"

"A cardinal," corrected Elizabeth. "You can tell from the sharp angle of his head."

"How do you know it's male?"

Elizabeth snatched the binoculars back. She wiped the lenses with the hem of her tweed coat. "I've been at this awhile."

"How about that." Abner scanned the trees. "Say, Elizabeth—are there any…" He trailed off.

"Any what?"

He bit his lip. "Please don't think I'm being stupid."

"I'm not in the habit of condescending to valedictorians," retorted Elizabeth.

"Salutatorian," mumbled Abner. "But, so… are there any… I mean, have you heard of any… I don't know… *large* birds?"

"Like a hawk?"

"Or maybe a… falcon?" He harrumphed. "Not a falcon. Even *bigger* than that."

"Like an albatross?"

"Maybe that big."

"In Massachusetts? Certainly not."

A shadow fell over Abner's face. The young man always looked anxious. He rarely smiled or laughed; his eyes often widened with confusion and fear, especially near students he didn't know well. His every step was clumsy, like a poorly strung marionette. But now he looked plaintive. Something troubled him.

"What's on your mind?" said Elizabeth, with forced cheeriness.

"Nothing," he said. "Just seeing things."

He turned away, down the track.

"Where are you going?" called Elizabeth.

"I just… I have to write a letter," he stuttered. "I'll see you later."

❖

When Miss Greyson entered the classroom, she cradled a clay cylinder in her arms. Students quieted at the sight of her, sat up straight. Miss Greyson crossed to the front, then heaved the object onto her wooden table. The cylinder looked like a milk jug, except for the spout that extended from its curved belly. Miss Greyson stepped away, straightened her dark blouse, and inspected her pupils.

No one spoke. Fifteen students gazed at the ceramic vessel, straining to read the tiny writing etched into its tan-colored surface.

"Who among you," said Miss Greyson, "has seen this before?"

No one breathed a word. But this was common. Miss Greyson often stupefied her classrooms. She was tall and trim, and her corseted gown accentuated the straightness of her posture. Her gray eyes shimmered; they could petrify anyone. And yet, when the students were alone in their dormitories, they whispered their agreement: Miss Greyson was also striking, an ageless beauty. Her lectures, delivered in a theatrical cant, could shake them to the core. Even Elizabeth felt sheepish in her presence.

One student raised a hand. An awkward young man with dirty-blond hair. Miss Greyson crooked a finger at him. "Yes, Mr. Dalton," she said. "Enlighten us."

"It's a Revigator, ma'am."

"Now *that's* a fancy name," said Miss Greyson. "So you've heard of it before. What does it do?"

"It's for health, ma'am."

"Is it? How so?"

"Well..." Dalton cleared his throat. He looked pleased with himself. "There's radium in the liner. You're supposed to fill it up overnight, and—well, you drink it, ma'am."

"Do I?" Miss Greyson pressed a hand to her bosom.

"Well, that is, not *you*, ma'am. But—my aunt has one. It helps her arthritis."

Miss Greyson nodded vaguely. Then she turned her head. Her eyes sliced through the bunch, straight to the back of the classroom.

"Miss *Crowne*," said Miss Greyson. "You look like you have an opinion on the matter."

Elizabeth fidgeted. What had she done? Rolled her eyes, probably. But how had Miss Greyson spotted her? Had her reaction really been so obvious? Elizabeth stopped twirling her pencil, arresting it in both hands.

"Penny for your thoughts, Miss Crowne?" Miss Greyson continued. The whole room shifted. Elizabeth could feel Abner's eyes on her. Everyone was staring now, wondering what she had to say. She saw two students chuckle into cupped hands.

Elizabeth shrugged. "I'm sure I don't know."

"You're *sure you don't know*," echoed Greyson. "Because you haven't *tested* it. You have no subjects. You have no methodology. You have no *information*. So how *could* you know?" Miss Greyson glared at her. Her lips bulged as she licked her teeth. "And yet—I think you have an educated guess. That is, I think you have an opinion, based on limited empirical evidence. Would that be so, Miss Crowne?"

Elizabeth's pulse pounded in her neck. She felt a drunken warmth swell inside her temples. At last she said, "I suppose I do."

Miss Greyson leaned back, pressing her palms against the table. She jutted her chin toward the Revigator.

"Well, then?" said Miss Greyson. "What do your instincts tell you, Miss Crowne?"

"My instincts tell me," said Elizabeth slowly, "that it's a sham."

The class broke into murmurs. Students leaned into each other. One shook his head. Elizabeth remembered why she never spoke in class—because of *this*. The whispers, the muffled snickering. Their doubt, their disdain. They resented her presence, and when she knew something they didn't, they resented her for showingboating. She wanted to trail off, to clam up. Nevertheless, she persisted.

"Radium is a dangerous element," she said. "It's nothing to be trifled with. Handling radium is known to cause burns and lesions. And anyway, Revigators put lead and arsenic in the water. And everybody knows they're poisonous. I don't see why anyone would use such a contraption."

"Well it worked for my aunt," huffed Dalton.

"I don't think it did."

Dalton craned his neck. He stared daggers at her. "*Pardon* me?"

"Pardon *me*," Elizabeth rejoined. "But I think the effect was placebo. It was all in her head. She believed she would feel better, so she did. But the chemistry is nonsense. It's quackery. And if I were her doctor…" Elizabeth swallowed. "I'd slap some sense into her."

"Well," spat Dalton, "you're *not* her doctor, are you? Or anyone else's, for that matter."

Elizabeth folded her arms. "I guess we're even, then."

With this final retort, Elizabeth sensed a sudden stillness. She wanted to say a hundred things just then—to claim she didn't know for sure, to insist that maybe she was wrong, to apologize for lecturing. But she added nothing. She only stiffened her lips, tightened the weave of her fingers, and waited for someone else to speak.

"Well, then," Miss Greyson said, at last. "Miss Crowne, I'll have to find you another gift for Christmas."

The professor spoke with a curled smile. Someone snickered; someone else chuckled. Soon the room was blossoming with laughter. Even Elizabeth smirked. Dalton, looking self-conscious, let himself giggle along.

And for a split-second, Elizabeth glimpsed Miss Greyson—she saw a *look*. But what was it? Approval? Amusement? Whatever it was, Elizabeth lit up like a sparkler. She liked the look, whatever it had meant, that flicker of acknowledgement. Then, as if nothing had happened, Miss Greyson turned to the blackboard, drew a piece of chalk, and began to scratch formulae into the slate.

❖

The key slipped from Elizabeth's hand and tinkled on the floor. She sighed, bent over, and picked it up with lifeless fingers. She was tired. She could barely find the energy to slip the key into its lock.

The door clinked shut. Elizabeth slumped against it, and she let her belt of books flump to the woven rug. Elizabeth scarcely registered the dusty texts piled on her hutch, the Underwood standing in the middle, and the crumpled typing paper scattered on the floor. Unlaundered clothes lay in heaps; stockings and scarves drooped from bed posts. Her quarters were already cramped; the disorder made them stifling.

Elizabeth crossed the room on rigid legs. She let her body collapse headlong into the unmade bed.

She might have remained there all evening, falling asleep in her clothes, neither bathed nor brushed. But then she heard a sound; something *crinkled* beneath her blanket. At first, Elizabeth smothered her face in the ruffled fabric. She wanted to ignore the figment sound. But then she rolled onto her side, peeled the blanket back, and saw the strips of paper underneath.

They were three clippings. The gray newsprint was creased, but the ink was clearly printed. The news stories weren't old, she could tell. Elizabeth lifted one, toward the afternoon sunlight that trickled between her curtains. She scanned the text, but before she could finish reading, she saw an indentation in the paper. She flipped the scrap over and saw a note, written in pencil: TONIGHT, BELL TOWER, 9 P.M.

❖

Abner bounced the ball against the floor. Sweat dripped from his nose. He watched the rubber sphere, contemplating its movement—up and down, floor to right hand, right hand to floor, floor to left hand. The ball traveled cleanly, tracing an orange triangle in the air.

Abner glanced up at his opponent. The other man was taller, his long arms coated in furry blond hair, like an albino ape. He splayed his body into a defensive X. From the bleachers, Abner looked no match for the gold-haired boy. Abner was shorter, more compact, his arm muscles lean and adolescent.

Suddenly, Abner dashed sideways. The other boy mirrored the movement, but Abner feinted, swiveled around, bounced the ball hard, and fired his shot. The ball arced majestically, then swished through the net. The other boy retrieved it, took his place on the edge of the court, and tried the same maneuver. Yet Abner was too quick; he smacked the ball away, chased it a few steps, regained control, and zigzagged across the floorboards. He leapt upward, and the ball seemed to float out of his hand, depositing itself in the hoop.

"Shucks!" yelled the towhead. He crossed the court, arms swinging. He snatched up his towel and shook his head. "I've said it before, Ab—you're wasting your time in the sticks. You should be trying out for the Celtics."

Abner found his own towel and patted down his nape. "If only," he murmured.

"You're good enough. Anybody can see that."

"Maybe one-on-one."

"You're too humble," said the towhead. "Say, doll, what do *you* think?"

Abner looked confused. *Doll?* He turned around and scanned the empty bleachers. There, tucked into a shadowy corner, sat Elizabeth. She perched on the polished wood plank, dressed in her coat and black beret, a mug pressed between her gloved hands.

"Do you think he's got the stuff?" called the towhead. "Maybe he ought to go pro?"

Elizabeth rose from her seat. "Looks like an expert to me," she said.

"*See*," said the towhead. He clapped Abner on the shoulder and tottered toward the exit.

The room felt hollow and dark. A single lamp hung from the ceiling, illuminating a circle on the court. Elizabeth wandered into the light. Her smile was warm, but strange.

"If I didn't know better," said Abner, stretching the towel over his shoulders, "I'd say you looked *fartrakht*."

"You say the sweetest things," Elizabeth replied, sipping from her mug.

"It means *pensive*."

Elizabeth nodded, watching the steam rise from her coffee. "Well, you *don't* know better, because I am very much *fartrakht*."

"Are you all right?" asked Abner, his voice softening. "Is there anything I can do?"

"Actually, there is."

"Oh? Sure! Just name it!"

"You can come with me to the bell tower."

"The bell tower?" Abner asked. "The one in the chapel?"

"Well, it's more *above* the chapel, but yes. I presume that's the one."

"What's... what's up there?"

Elizabeth grimaced. "I don't know, actually. That's why I want you along."

It was strange, watching Abner transform. On the court, he was unstoppable. His dexterous body sashayed past rival players, and the ball seemed to dribble itself. When he took his shots, the ball never grazed the basket's rim; it eased soundlessly through. Yet the moment Abner stepped back into real life, he lost his athletic vim. He collapsed into himself. His very soul started to palsy.

"When?"

"Nine o'clock. So you have just enough time to shower and change."

"I don't know." Abner rubbed a palm against his stubbled cheek. "I have an exam tomorrow."

"*Abner*," Elizabeth chided.

Hearing his name was all it took. He fled to the showers, and ten minutes later he was dressed in bulbous layers of winter clothes.

"I'm not going to regret this, am I?" he asked.

"Have you ever regretted spending time with me?"

To this, Abner had no response. They proceeded silently through the door, into the dark and frigid quad.

❖

Elizabeth had rarely stepped inside the campus chapel. She blamed her family for this; her mother was a twice-a-year Anglican, and her father hadn't entered a Presbyterian Church since boyhood. Elizabeth admired the chapel's architecture, its century-old stonework and crenellated tower. Yet the chapel meant little to her. It stood in an awkward nook of campus, far from classrooms or dormitories.

As they reached the beveled red doors, Abner stammered, "Can you at least tell me what this is all about?"

Elizabeth paused on the chapel's steps. "Someone invited me here."

"Who?"

"I don't know. But whoever it was, he gave me three newspaper clippings."

"Newspaper clippings? What about?"

Elizabeth hesitated. "Have you ever heard of Saint Majella's Abbey?"

Abner rubbed his chin with mittoned fingers. "Isn't that… somewhere nearby?"

"It's about twenty miles away," confirmed Elizabeth. "It's a place for Trappistine nuns."

"Trappist-who?"

"Trappis*tine*. Dreary bunch, from what I hear. You could say they're the nuns with the longest rulers."

"Well—what about them?"

"It seems they've had some problems."

Abner hedged. "An outbreak?"

"You could say that."

"Of what? The grip?"

Elizabeth groped the iron handle and pushed inside. "Of *murder*."

The nave was silent and dark, except for the glow of votive candles. A carved statue of the Virgin Mary loomed above the altar; an emaciated Christ languished in her lap. Elizabeth crossed to a narrow door; she slipped through, into a spiral staircase. The twisting passage was pitch black, and it only took an instant for Abner to stub his toe on an unseen step.

"*Ow,*" he whined. "Don't you have a light?"

"Unless I've missed my guess," Elizabeth said, "there should be one above us."

Elizabeth reached the top. As she expected, a warm glow seeped into the stairwell, outlining a rectangle in the ceiling. Elizabeth pushed open the trapdoor, climbed the final steps, and found herself in a dusty attic. Abner followed; he peeked his head through the floor, surveyed the shadowy walls, and drew a breath of surprise.

"Professor..." he spluttered. "Professor *O'Malley?*"

Dr. O'Malley sat at a card table. A kerosene lantern burned next to him, casting his face in orange. His expression was calm; he pulled back the sleeves of his thick wool sweater, reached toward a teapot, and poured into two ceramic cups.

"Good evening, Elizabeth," Dr. O'Malley said gently. "And—Mr. Cohen, is it not?"

"Me?" whispered Abner. "Yes, sir."

"I'm sure Miss Crowne appreciates your courage," said Dr. O'Malley, "but you needn't linger. This is to be a private conversation. And you have my word I'm no threat to her."

Most of Abner's body was still inside the staircase; only his face and hat were visible above the open trap. His eyes darted from Elizabeth to the professor. At last his friend said, "It's fine, Abner. Thank you for escorting me."

"You're sure?"

Elizabeth shot a look at Dr. O'Malley. "*Am* I sure?"

Dr. O'Malley smiled bemusedly. "If Elizabeth doesn't knock on your door at 7 o'clock tomorrow morn, ring the police station in town."

"All... all right, then," Abner murmured. He sank into the floor and disappeared. Elizabeth could barely hear his faint call, "Goodnight, Elizabeth!"

Elizabeth seated herself in the empty folding chair. She touched the rim of her teacup. "*Sláinte,*" she said.

Dr. O'Malley leaned back. "And cheers to you."

Elizabeth sipped the bland liquid. "So what are we toasting, professor? If you're conscripting me for the Fenian cause, you should know I don't have a drop of Irish blood."

The man's smile broadened. As he plucked up his

spectacles and slipped them over his ears, Elizabeth studied her professor. Dr. O'Malley was new to Saint Luke's—he'd only started that same semester—and she had never really *looked* at him before. He was young, for an academic. He was also a beanpole; his cheekbones were sharp and angular. He crossed his long legs and rested one arm on the back of his chair. His scarf was unfastened and draped over his bony shoulders. As ever, his hair was slicked to one side. His specs were small and rectangular, decorated with little curls of wire. Perhaps it was his Celtic fashion or his tranquil demeanor, but somehow Elizabeth had missed how raffish the man appeared.

"I have a theory," said Dr. O'Malley, drawing a pipe from his satchel. "I think you are fond of medicine. I see you have a talent for it. But try as you might, you have never pictured yourself a physician."

Elizabeth's eyes dropped to the table. "How come?"

Dr. O'Malley struck a match and inserted the flame. Tobacco crackled.

"There is no question of your skill," said Dr. O'Malley through webs of smoke. "A duller man might think you shy. But what I see is not a timid girl. Quite the opposite. I think, Miss Crowne, that you are *bored*."

Elizabeth bristled. She blinked at Dr. O'Malley, but a long pause followed, and she looked away again.

"You needn't say so," continued Dr. O'Malley, his voice still soothing. "But I think I'm right. For yes, if you ever found yourself in the surgical theatre, I think you'd capably wield a scalpel. You could sew a wound without much practice. And in a few years, God willing, you could open a clinic, or make house calls, or play midwife to expectant mothers. One day, your peers might see past your sex, and they might even refer some patients. And if that's what you desire, then godspeed,

Miss Crowne, for it is a noble calling, and you're a brave lass to spend your time here, outshining all these parvenus."

Dr. O'Malley paused again. This was her chance. She could do anything in that moment—crack a joke, storm away, object to his presumptions. Yet she didn't. She felt immobile, mute, lashed to her seat. She could barely summon the voice to reply, "But?"

A sly grin slinked across Dr. O'Malley's lips. Then it was lost in a gust of smoke.

"What did you think of those newspaper clippings?"

"Morose," said Elizabeth.

"Murder generally is."

"And," she added quickly, "I can't say I appreciate strange men sneaking into my quarters while I'm out."

Dr. O'Malley nodded. "Fair. And not to be repeated. But now that the deed is done—can you deny you were intrigued?"

"What do you think intrigued me?"

Abbess Falls from St. Majella's Window

3 Weeks, 3 Mysterious Deaths, Police Baffled

QUENTIN COUNTY: Anguish was renewed at St. Majella's Abbey, where Reverend Mother Meredith McMurty, 71, was discovered in the central court, struck dead by a three-story fall.

In the wake of similar tragedies, police continue to investigate the Trappistine Abbey, where three deaths have now been reported in as many weeks. One detective has been called from as far away as Springfield to provide his expertise.

In the two prior cases, one nun was found asphyxiated in her quarters, while a second was stabbed repeatedly with a pitchfork in the communal garden. Neither case produced witnesses or signs of intrusion.

Castleboro police are offering a reward of $100 for any information leading to the arrest of credible suspects.

"Let's review the facts." Dr. O'Malley stood up. Pacing, he rubbed his chin with a free hand. "The scene is Saint Majella's Abbey. The time is night. A nun is asleep in her cell. She's old, more than eighty years. Her senses are dull. She can't hear well. Her weak old gams can't run, if ever they could."

"She's a sitting duck," said Elizabeth.

"If," added Dr. O'Malley, "someone enters her chambers. And then—someone does. Late at night. A killer sneaks inside. Grabs her throat. Holds it tight. Squeezes the life from her. She has but one defense—her voice—and that is smothered. Her death is absolutely silent." Dr. O'Malley curled his lip, then shrugged. "A sitting duck, as you say. A child could've done it."

"Except..."

Dr. O'Malley raised a pinky. "Except?"

"The door was locked," said Elizabeth. "She had no closet. There was no place to hide."

"Then what's the simplest answer?"

"Someone had a key."

"Ah," sighed Dr. O'Malley. "Of course. A master key, perhaps. Which points to what suspect?"

"Someone inside the convent. Another nun."

Dr. O'Malley pressed the stem of his pipe against his forehead. "What if I told you there is no master key. There are no copies. Just suppose, for now, we remove it from this equation. What then?"

"It's an old convent?" asked Elizabeth. "At least a hundred years, I'm guessing?"

"Oh, at least."

"That rules out an air duct. And the police would have found a secret passage."

"Certainly they would. Stumped yet?"

Elizabeth started to pour herself a second cup of tea. "But there were two more clippings. That is—two more murders."

"Then let's proceed," said Dr. O'Malley. "Three days later. A second nun is alone in the garden. The walls are high. The doors are closed. It's the middle of the day. It's late autumn, so nothing is growing. Why is she there?"

Elizabeth waved a hand. "Who can say?"

"Perhaps she wants to be alone," said Dr. O'Malley. "To meditate. She finds it peaceful, among the dead tomato plants. Perhaps she *watches birds*."

Elizabeth shifted uncomfortably. Was this an innocent guess? Or did Dr. O'Malley know something about her pastimes? "Fine," she said. "The nun likes the garden. It's a—what?—a sanctuary."

"It *is* a sanctuary. Or it always has been—until someone appears. A killer. Out of nowhere. The nun is ambushed. Cornered. She's only sixty years, but still it's hard for her to run. She screams—too late. The killer snatches a pitchfork from the wall. Drives it through her. The tines skewer her flesh. Twenty puncture wounds. No witnesses, but—her sisters are nearby. Standing in the court. They hear her wails of pain. They rush to the garden door. And what do they find? The weapon. The nun, lying in a pool of blood. But nothing else. No sign of an intruder. How could this be?"

"I don't suppose it was suicide," grumbled Elizabeth. "No other exit?"

"The garden is enclosed. The outer walls are ten feet high, and the dividing wall is higher. I've seen it myself. There's no way out."

"Well, you've got me again," said Elizabeth. "Unless I'm to believe in ghosts."

Dr. O'Malley sniffed. "Let's move on, then. The third incursion."

"Yes, about that," said Elizabeth. "I couldn't follow the last one. The article was vague."

"The third," said Dr. O'Malley. "The strangest of all. Three nights later. By now, the nuns are terrified. They fear for their lives. Two of their sisters have perished, and no one knows how. They pray, of course—surely this is the Devil's work—but they are practical as well. They walk in groups. They observe an early curfew. They sleep two to a cell, so no one is ever alone."

"Except," said Elizabeth, "the Mother Superior."

"The Mother Superior," echoed O'Malley. "*She* spends time alone. In fact, she is often alone. The night in question, the Mother Superior hides in her study. Her most trusted sisters guard the door. It is the only door, and it is locked from the inside. The nuns guard this door in shifts. There is only the one way in. The study is the uppermost room, in the fourth story of the abbey's tallest building. Where could she be safer?"

"But someone got in," said Elizabeth.

"Yet how? Again, no wardrobe, no cupboard, nowhere to hide. Night falls. The abbess is alone. The nuns stand guard, too afraid to doze. All of a sudden, someone cries out. They hear a commotion—a slam, a crash, and then the words: *You! You're the one who did it!* The guards bang on the door, but they can't get in. They have no spare key. They can only listen as their Mother Superior struggles inside. She screams and screams. They hear her voice, traveling across the room. Pulled. Against her will. And then they hear a final cry—loud at first, then receding into silence. But you know the reason for that."

"Because she fell," croaked Elizabeth. "She fell out the window."

"No," corrected Dr. O'Malley. "She was *thrown* from the window. She fell four stories and crashed through the roof of a toolshed. When they found her, her bones were splinters."

"No ladder?" said Elizabeth. "No fire escape? No other entrance?"

"None at all."

"What was inside? If there was a struggle, then…"

"A fine question," said Dr. O'Malley. He tapped his pipe against a beam, letting the ashes spill to the floor. He ground their embers into the boards and blew into the pipe's bowl. "What did the nuns find, once they'd broken down the door? A simple table, where the abbess wrote and prayed. Papers cast about the floor. An overturned inkwell. A candelabra, knocked over and burned out. There was still light, thanks to the sconces, but little else." He smirked. "Convents aren't well furnished."

"How far from the table to the window?"

"The room is sizeable. Fifteen feet, give or take."

"Then someone dragged her."

"Indeed. There were boot prints on the table. But there was a strange thing—there were only two."

"Two—boot prints?"

"Precisely. Right in the middle of the table." O'Malley took a long breath. He leaned back in the chair pursed his lips. "My theory is this: If Elizabeth Crowne spent fifty years in a hospital ward, she would die an ambivalent old woman. But if she solved this riddle, she would die tomorrow a happy girl. There is nothing in the world of medicine that holds a candle to a mystery such as this. And if I'm right, I will gladly seek your help."

"But why me?" Elizabeth demanded.

Dr. O'Malley raised a finger to his temple. "I'll tell you, Elizabeth. I promise. But only when the time is right."

"But where would I even start?" Elizabeth persisted. "If the police can't find the culprit, how am I supposed to?"

"Ah, that's the thing," said Dr. O'Malley. "You needn't find the culprit."

"No? Why not?"

"Because I already know who it is. The question isn't *who*. It's not even why. What I want to know—is *how*."

❖

Elizabeth sat at her desk, watching equations appear. The chalk scratched its way across the blackboard, an ever-expanding cloud of digits and letters, and Elizabeth struggled to transcribe what she saw. True, these kinds of formulae always made her cross-eyed, but Elizabeth was also distracted. She kept watching the tightly wrapped bun on top of her professor's head. She saw the shoulders shake with every jot of the chalk. She traced the voluptuous curve of Miss Greyson's back, the slight swish of her black dress. As she wrote, Miss Greyson's second arm was akimbo against her hip, like a flamenco dancer.

Could she really be a murderer?

Elizabeth felt a pressure in her forehead. With her free hand, she absently twisted strands of hair around her finger. Yes, Miss Greyson had a penetrating presence; her eyes were fierce, her mouth was mocking, even her dark dresses were severely fashioned. But she did not seem cruel. She had never degraded her students, never insulted their intelligence. In truth, she captivated them. She lashed out questions like a cracking whip. She strode about the room in figure-eights, tantalizing the young men with her incandescence. If Miss Greyson was a cold-blooded murderess, then anyone could be.

Suddenly, Miss Greyson twirled around. The students leaned back, surprised by her movement. She studied her pupils, then slapped her chalk on the table.

"*Why* do we do this?" she purred. She inspected the room, brushing a finger across her lips.

"Why... why do we do what?" someone cheeped.

"Why chemistry? Why study these strings of numbers?"

The only sound was a gust of wet wind rattling the windowsills.

"I'll tell you why *I* do it." Miss Greyson turned her head to the blackboard. She touched the chalk markings with the tips of her fingers. "I find them beautiful. Perhaps you think that odd. How could numbers be beautiful? Look at this one—a delta, just a little triangle." She gazed at them tenderly. "Well—what you see up here is *life*. Nitrogen and oxygen combine to make the air you breathe. Hydrogen and oxygen make the water you drink. Oxygen and carbon make—*us*." She turned halfway, not quite facing them. "These numbers are *you*. Your body. Your blood. Your thoughts are chemistry. Your *soul* is chemistry. These exchanges make you what you are."

Miss Greyson moved toward the window. Tree branches swayed in the gathering wind, and specs of snow raced past the glass.

"Remember that," she said. "Dull as they may seem, these numbers are the shorthand of your existence. You have but one life. Understanding what you are is the greatest gift there is." She sniffed, rubbed her arm, and said, "I think that's enough for today."

"Do we have an assignment?" squeaked a voice.

"Yes," said Miss Greyson. "If the snow sticks—I want you to build a snowman."

The students exchanged looks. Then they allowed themselves to chuckle. They clapped their books shut, gathered their coats and bags, and filed out of the room.

Elizabeth felt queasy. She slid away from her desk and collected her things. But before she could reach the door, she heard Miss Greyson speak: "Miss Crowne, a moment of your time?"

Elizabeth turned back to her professor. Miss Greyson still faced the window, but Elizabeth could see her own reflection in the glass—an opaque outline, a profile lacking definition, small compared to Miss Greyson's daunting figure. Elizabeth swelled with shame. What was she even doing? Had she really agreed to spy on her professor? To catalogue her movements? All because of a cockamamie accusation, told to her in private by an Irish physician she barely knew?

The room had emptied. Miss Greyson said, "I met your father once."

Elizabeth was startled. "Oh?"

"At a symposium. He was lecturing on physics. You're probably tired of hearing how brilliant he is."

Elizabeth cradled her books tighter.

"He's also a good man," Miss Greyson added. She leaned a shoulder against the windowsill, still watching the snow. The thick flakes were falling in earnest. "You and I have that in common. We were raised by decent fathers." She tapped her fingertips together. "I wouldn't blame you for being anxious."

Elizabeth cleared her throat. "How do you mean?"

"Before me," Miss Greyson said, "there were three women who taught among these halls. One taught algebra. Another taught nutrition. The third taught how to dress wounds. That last one had served as a nurse during the Civil War. Old and feisty. She could break a wild stallion if she wanted to. I admired her the most—but I respected them all. This is a school full of men. Men who like to play god. They have no patience for women." She glanced at Elizabeth. "Yet here you are. The first. As a female student, you have no predecessors. And no one knows what to make of you. You're too bright to bully. You're too headstrong to woo. What is a young man to do with you? So they do nothing. They ignore you. They pretend you don't exist."

"Not all of them," Elizabeth mumbled.

"You must mean Abner Cohen," scoffed Miss Greyson. "Your friend, I gather. A Jew with a basketball scholarship. They're a dime a dozen, you know. Or a dime for *two* dozen, if they got their way. But you—*you* are different, and will always be. I know this, because we have something else in common."

Elizabeth sighed. "I know what you're saying. We—"

"*We're unafraid of truth.*" Miss Greyson pulled herself away from the window. She went to the table to arrange her scattered papers. "A hundred thousand housewives would drink that radiated water, just because some salesman told them to. A hundred thousand more would lobotomize their children, or coat themselves in snake oil, or swallow a handful of sugar pills. But *you* would not."

Miss Greyson bundled the papers and strode toward the door. Then she stopped. "I didn't want you here. I even told the chancellor. I thought it was nepotism. *Dr. Crowne's daughter,*

I thought. *Of course they'd let her in.* But that wasn't it at all. I see that now. And I'm glad that I was wrong."

With that, Miss Greyson quit the room, leaving Elizabeth alone.

❖

Elizabeth pressed her palms against her face, squishing her cheeks together. Her elbows rested on the study carol's flat surface. She stared blankly at the text beneath her, but Elizabeth wasn't reading. She was lost in thought, having long forgotten she was in the school library, in the loneliest corner, besieged by stacks of reference books.

"*Elizabeth!*" came a whisper.

She jolted upright, alarmed by her own name. "Abner, what are you doing here?"

"We have to talk," he said.

Abner knelt down beside her. He breathed heavily; his cheeks were flushed. He had clearly run here, and the buttons of his coat were fastened in the wrong holes. His hat lay askew over disheveled hair.

"Fine," said Elizabeth, crossing her arms.

"May I sit down?"

"Go! Sit! It's not *my* library."

Abner dragged a chair from a nearby table and placed it next to Elizabeth. She angled her own chair sideways, so they could sit face to face. They leaned toward each other awkwardly, their voices hushed.

"So what is it?" said Elizabeth.

"I was just at practice," began Abner. "We finished, and I went to the showers. The boys were talking. And one of them—do you know Riley?"

"The scrawny red-haired boy?"

"That's him. Anyway, he said he'd *seen* something. The other night, he stepped outside for a cigarette. He wanted to see the moon, which was almost full. Do you remember?"

"Yes, yes. So what happened?"

"Well, he was standing near the dining hall. But on the north side, closer to the woods. And when he looked up—he saw something in the sky."

"What kind of something?"

"He said he saw a woman."

"A *what?*"

"I know it sounds crazy. The other boys made fun of him. But Riley, he couldn't stop himself. He's such an earnest kid. He said he saw the shape of a woman—flying through the sky. And it was a clear night. The moon was so bright. He said he saw her clearly…"

Abner faltered. He took off his hat and wiped his brow with the back of his hand. As he did this, a memory flickered in Elizabeth's mind.

"*You* saw the same thing, didn't you?" When Abner didn't respond, she said, "*That's* why you asked me about large birds. You saw a *woman in the sky*, and you thought—you thought you were *seeing things*."

"It was the same night," Abner murmured. "I was in my room. My window faces north—just where Riley saw…" Abner covered his face in his hands. "I just keep thinking, if I've lost my mind, Riley must have, too."

"A woman in the sky," Elizabeth said to herself. "Abner—I'm asking you this in strict confidence. Can I trust you?"

Abner frowned. "Well, geez, Liz—do you really have to ask?"

"Of course, of course. I'm sorry, Ab. It's just—this is important. And no one can know. Do you know where Miss Greyson lives?"

"Miss Greyson? Our chemistry teacher?"

"Exactly. Does she live on campus?"

"I don't think so." Abner thought a moment, then raised his eyebrows. "Wait—I think she lives on Dayton Road. A couple miles down. I forget why I know that, but one of the other boys was joking about it, because her name rhymes. *Miss Greyson of Dayton...*"

"Does she have a car? A horse?"

"Now that you mention it, I don't think she does. I think she hops a ride with Mister Michaels. He's a milkman, has a dairy farm not too far from here..."

Elizabeth squeezed Abner's arm. "Thank you for telling me this. Suffice it to say, you're *not* crazy. Neither is Riley. But let's keep this between us, all right?"

"But what *is* it?" Abner pleaded. "Does it have something to do with—you know—that meeting you had..."

"Let's talk about it later," interrupted Elizabeth. "Right now, I need to find a bicycle."

Abner raised an eyebrow inquisitively. "What if I could find *two?*"

❖

Henrietta Greyson could not decide whether to eat her apple. She was peckish, yes, but this apple was such a perfect red sphere; it fit her fingers so snugly. She leaned into the spokes of her swivel chair and studied its perfect shape, the unnatural gleam of its skin in the subdued morning light. One bite would ruin that smooth surface, exposing the white flesh beneath.

The apple would turn brown in a matter of minutes. How unjust it was.

She looked past the apple, at the papers scattered over her desk. She sighed at the piles of ungraded homework— jumbled numbers, Cartesian graphs, the half-understood axes of ambivalent mathematicians. Above her desk, the window panes beaded with moisture, obscuring her view of the campus' central court. The day was gray, and the rooftops and foothills blended together.

Such grisly weather, she thought. *I should be home now. No one should have to leave her living room when the weather's like this.*

A tap on her door roused Henrietta from her reverie. She sat up straight and rotated toward the entrance. In the doorway stood two figures: The first was a man, medium-sized and mustached, with tiny round spectacles. He removed his feathered homburg, revealing thin, gray hair. His other hand was pressed against the shoulder of a boy.

"Good morning," said Henrietta. "How may I help you gentlemen?"

She directed the question not at the man, but the boy. He was small and rosy-cheeked, and his tight-fitting trousers revealed the skinniness of his legs. The rest of him was covered in a bulky brown coat and loosely tied scarf. His face was barely visible beneath the brim of an oversized deerstalker.

"Forgive us, miss," said the man. "I'm a little turned-around. Do you know where to find the office of Dr. Jenson?"

Henrietta felt a quiver beneath her eye. She felt heat burn through her body, like the rekindled coals of a campfire. She gazed at the boy, his little patch of face framed in layers of wool.

"And what's your name?" Henrietta murmured to the boy.

The man straightened his shoulders impatiently. He said, "Answer the lady's question, Archie."

The boy's eyes dropped to the tiles. "Archibald Wakefield, ma'am."

"And how old are you?"

"Miss, I apologize," said the man, "but we're a bit pressed for time."

Henrietta felt her pulse everywhere—in her wrists, in her neck, and most of all, pounding in her chest. Air seeped through her nostrils. When she swallowed, she heard her throat crackle. Even her tongue dragged tensely against the roof of her mouth.

"You're a very handsome boy, Archie," said Henrietta. "I'd adore to have a child like you."

And then, just as the man opened his mouth, Henrietta turned and said, "One flight down, room two-twelve. It's the only green door. You shan't miss it."

The man clapped his jaw shut. He grimaced and bowed his chin, then ushered Archie away.

"Much obliged, miss."

Henrietta said, "*Professor.*"

The man paused in mid-step. "I'm sorry?"

"I am a professor of physics and higher maths," said Henrietta.

The man adjusted his spectacles. He forced himself to grin. "Ah," he said. "Well, then. Good day."

The two figures vanished, leaving the door frame empty.

Henrietta reached to her desk. She grasped a pencil. She held it in the air. She twirled it around with her fingers. Her eyes burned. For a moment, she wondered whether she could suppress the wave of emotion. But it was coming. She could feel it. The walls of her office warped inward; the ceiling weighed down.

The Fury.

That familiar fire in her belly. It coursed inside her. She took deep drafts of air; she focused on the desk, the walls, her small bookcase packed with volumes, but still, they melted away. The Fury consumed everything. It made everything else invisible. And soon her eyes welled up with memory—

—she remembered the cell. She could picture herself there, even now, all these years later. The thin straw mattress. The plain wood cross, nailed to a stone wall. The tiny window that shed so little light. The curdled stench of the chamber pot, stashed beneath her bunk and shared with a dozen other girls. The cold that seeped through her ragged nightgown. Even now, her fingers coiled with the memory of that scrub-brush; her back still felt the relentless ache of bent-over toil. She touched her hair, dug through its thick brown tresses, massaged her scalp. Henrietta could still feel where her hair had been yanked, when the Sisters had dragged her across the floor. She could still sense the tingle of saliva on her cheeks, where the Sisters spat on her. She could still wince, the way she had always winced, at the slurs the Sisters had flung at her. *Harlot. Hussy. Slut.*

Henrietta looked at her hand. She groped the pencil tight. Her knuckles trembled, and her blue veins strained beneath ivory skin. The graphite point faced downward. She held the implement like a dagger.

It's happening again, she thought—or perhaps she whispered it aloud, she couldn't tell. She was entranced, just like all those times before. The Fury took hold of her, and it wouldn't let go. It demanded action. It demanded blood. She pictured herself rising from this chair, floating through the door, and stalking down the hall. She would follow the man in the homburg hat. She would raise that pencil over him. Yet it would not be *she* who brandished the pencil, but the Fury. The same Fury that the nuns had cultivated all those months. The Fury they had sown and harvested, with every thwack of their paddles. They had ripped away her womanhood and replaced it with the Fury, and that is why she would wait—until the man turned around, curious, surprised, to see Henrietta behind him. His eyes would bulge with disbelief, but too late. Henrietta would drive the pencil down, into his impotent body. The Fury would slash through him, and Henrietta would watch, disembodied, as the man crumpled to her feet.

I can't stay here, she thought.

Henrietta slammed the pencil to her desk. She rose and adjusted her blouse. She tore her coat from its peg.

Suddenly, Henrietta heard the clang of a bell. The noise jostled her; she leaned against the bookcase. She glanced out the window and identified its source—the church bell rang in its steeple, just as it did every hour.

Her eyes traced the shape of the church. Her gaze dropped down the slate roof, the open doorway, and the stone steps. She saw the lawn, a patchwork of pale green and puddles of mud.

Then she saw it: a buggy. The vehicle was parked in the middle of the yard, its seat covered in a black canopy. Beside it stood a gray-bearded man, wearing a thick duster and a broad hat. He patted the faces of the buggy's two horses, then waved to a passerby.

Dr. Ridge, she thought. *He'll be out making house calls. He'll give me a ride. He'll take me home. He'll save me from the Fury.*

Miss Greyson stormed out of her office, not stopping to even shut the door.

❖

The road curved around the mountain. Walls of evergreens eased past them on either side. Abner's borrowed bike was small, but he had no trouble pedaling it; his thick boots rotated beneath him as the dirt surface whisked past. But he frowned at Elizabeth, who struggled to keep pace. Her front wheel wobbled over potholes and trenches; the front tire slammed into pebbles, throwing her off-balance. Abner was too polite to find this funny, but he did wonder how such a prodigious girl could be so incapable of riding in a straight line.

Forest dominated the landscape, and clouds covered the sky. The flurries hadn't stuck, but the air felt wintry all the same. There was little sign of human life, except for the endless line of utility poles festooned with cable. A curl of dark smoke dispersed above the trees, and Abner whiffed a wood stove through his clotted nose. Only once did they pass another person—a farmer waving from his wagon, pulled by a sulky pair of draft horses.

Had they biked any faster, Abner might have missed the opening in the trees. They turned onto a stony lot, barren except for a stack of firewood. The cottage was nestled in tree branches, its walls composed of logs and mortar. The slate roof sagged, and moss bulged from every tile. The stone chimney was dormant. The windows were covered. Never had Abner seen a home so bereft of life.

"She lives *here?*" Abner wondered aloud. "It's so lonely."

"Maybe it's cheerier in the spring," offered Elizabeth.

They pushed their bicycles into the woods and leaned them discreetly against a maple. Their boots sloshed through the carpet of leaves, where they stubbed their toes on hidden tree roots.

At the front door, Elizabeth dug inside her beret and removed a bobby pin. She held it squarely in front of her nose, pinched one end, and yanked it into a sharp angle. She knelt, inserted the pin, and rooted inside the lock. She listened for that satisfying *click*, and the door fell away from its frame.

"How did you do that?" Abner asked breathlessly.

"My mother," said Elizabeth, dusting off her skirt. "My father has a habit of misplacing keys. And my mother would rather die than pay for a locksmith. Give the woman a sewing needle and she could break out of Sing Sing."

Inside, the cottage was in better condition: The walls were composed of firm wood planks, and two high-backed chairs flanked an old davenport. A stone hearth took up the corner, its blackened logs smelling of last night's fire. Framed watercolors of forests and rivers were evenly spaced along the walls. An open passage led to the kitchen. The den felt cozy, lived-in, a place that anyone could call home.

"*Good God!*"

Elizabeth whirled around. Abner was pressed against the wall; a hand covered his heaving chest. She followed his terrified gaze to the window. The white curtains were like tissue paper, revealing the silhouette of cat.

The cat was enormous, easily fifteen pounds, and a fluffy mane enshrouded its head. But it was not the cat's size or feral coat that unnerved Elizabeth; rather, the cat wore a floral blue dress. The shoulders were bunched, and the skirt was pleated. Ribbons had been tied around the cat's ears, the loops dog-eared and misshapen. It looked like a doll. Or a little girl.

The sound of mewling drew her attention from the window. Two more cats rounded the corner from the kitchen, also costumed. One was dressed in a sailor suit, another in a white gown. A fourth brushed Abner's ankle, causing him to yelp. It was an orange tabby, its hind legs clad in leather chaps, a tiny cowboy hat dragging behind.

"I suppose everyone needs a hobby," Elizabeth muttered. "Now I wonder where *that* goes."

She pointed to a rustic door, wedged between the fireplace and a loaded bookshelf. She groped the handle and pulled. A staircase emerged, descending into a shadowy void.

"If I were a deadly secret," said Elizabeth, "I'd probably be down there."

She produced a matchbox and skinny wax candle from her coat pocket. The scent of burning phosphorous filled the air as the wick began to glow.

"Shall we?" said Elizabeth, inching toward the precipice.

Abner prickled all over. His veins ran cold. Elizabeth took her first step, and the squeal of rotten wood sent shivers through his body. He realized he was backing away, toward the front door.

Elizabeth turned and scowled. "You're not leaving me already?"

"No... I... see... I just..." Abner squeezed his eyes shut. "I'm claustrophobic."

"Dear lord," Elizabeth muttered.

"It's true! If I'm in a confined space for even a second, I just... I panic, Liz. I lose all my senses. I really do."

"You could have told me that."

"How was I supposed to know we were going into a cellar?"

"Never mind. Why don't you keep watch, then?"

"Okay," he assented.

Abner dug his hands into his pockets. He felt defeated. Why had he even come, if he was just going to dawdle in the living room? He felt as useless here as he had at home in Brooklyn. How many nights had he spent reading school books at the kitchen table while his father toiled at the shoe store? How many years had he tiptoed around his mother, who spent her good days ironing clothes and smoking cigarettes by the radio? Then, on the bad days, how often had he fled to the street, anything to get away from the shouting? How much had his basketball scholarship shocked everyone he knew? In all his years of practice on the neighborhood courts, neither parent, nor any of his four siblings, had any idea that Abner was such a gifted athlete. The morning he'd left his family on the platform at Grand Central Station had been the happiest moment of Abner's life.

Yet here he was, a coward. Wringing his hands in an empty room. A pack of harmless cats ambled around his ankles. Even the heartache he felt for Elizabeth—that plucky *shiksa*—couldn't make him brave. He was useless to her, a bashful middle child who played ball for a living. Really, he should just leave.

"By the way, Abner!" Elizabeth called from below. Her voice sounded hollow, coming from the middle of the dark staircase. "Not a lot of people get away with calling me Liz."

"Oh," Abner called down, silently castigating himself. "I'm sorry."

"Don't be. I like when *you* say it."

Abner was dumbstruck. A giddy warmth welled up inside him. He eased himself onto the sofa, rubbing his knees for warmth. That was the first compliment Elizabeth had ever paid him. Or *was* it a compliment? That was the trouble with Elizabeth, the snag that frustrated him most of all: Her words were never simple. Everything she said was brusque, barbed, qualified. Sometimes he felt like Elizabeth was talking to herself, and he was only eavesdropping. Yet she had never turned him away, as so many others had. She wasn't like the young men in the dining hall, who talked closely among themselves, ignoring Abner until he got bored and wandered away. Elizabeth let him tag along. Wasn't he her sidekick, her confidante? And now, for the first time, hadn't she let him use a private nickname? Couldn't he call her something no one else could? It was Liz, now. He would never call her *Elizabeth* again, not as long as he lived.

Abner heard a sound—the faint clop of hooves.

He turned to the window, peeled back the curtain. There, in front of the house, two horses emerged from the nettles. They pulled a covered black buggy.

He sprang to the cellar door. He threw it open and called, "Elizabeth! Someone's here!"

Far below, the candlelight was a nebulous glow in the darkness. Abner couldn't make out precise shapes, but he could tell Elizabeth wasn't moving in any direction.

Abner heard the clack of the buggy door opening. The sound of cordial conversation. He recognized the voice of Miss Greyson. Someone had driven her here. But why so soon? Wasn't she supposed to be in class? Was there a change in schedule? Was she ill? Whatever the case, she was here now, and she was coming inside.

Abner called again: "*Elizabeth!* We have to go, *now!*"

A cat leapt toward the window. The others scampered across the floor. One scratched at the base of the door, as if willing its master to come through it. Abner could barely breathe. He could see the man inside the buggy, his beard and top hat. The driver waved a final salute, then whipped at the horses, causing them to canter sideways. The vehicle maneuvered around, heading back to the road. Abner heard the tinkle of keys, the click of the lock.

Abner spun around. He grabbed the cellar door and slammed it shut. It banged into place.

Abner could sense the hesitation outside. Surely Miss Greyson had heard him. That was diversion enough. He darted across the rug, around the corner, and into the kitchen. He flew past the dining table, the cupboards, the counter, the dangling pots and pans, the stack of burlap sacks. He reached the far end of the house, nearly clipping the china cabinet. He grabbed the door handle, threw back the deadbolt, and hurled himself outside.

But he didn't see the steps. His first foot dropped too far. His second foot rammed his heel. He tumbled face-first into the leaves. His legs scrambled. He slipped on slick soil.

Then he heard the voice: *"Mister Cohen."*

He rolled over, face-up. Damp cold seeped into his shoulder blades.

Miss Greyson stood in the open doorway. She loomed over Abner. Her velveteen black dress shimmered in the dull light.

Abner wanted to explain himself. He could have improvised a lie, if he just had time to think. Words spilled through his mind.

Then he saw Miss Greyson's eyes. Steely. Half-closed. No emotion at all—no sympathy, no curiosity, not even confusion. Only judgment. Resolution.

Words would be useless. There was no choice. He must escape.

Abner clambered to his feet. He sprinted down the hill, deeper into the forest. He bolted through a stand of birch trees; skinny white trunks flashed past him. He barged through a briar bush. The thorns raked his body, catching on the fabric of his coat. He screeched in pain. Still he pressed forward. His boots thumped against the ground.

At last, he slowed. He pressed his back against a tree, heaving in the thin air. He looked back, toward the cottage. The building was only a gray blotch in the distance. He had run a hundred yards, at least. There was no chance that Miss Greyson could catch up to him. She no longer stood in the rear doorway. She must have gone inside. Surely, he was safe.

Then it happened—Abner saw movement. Her heard the crackle of branches. He looked up.

The shape was human. Sailing sideways through the air. One leg extended forward. The other bent behind. Like a figure skater. Breeze rippled through her dress. Her hat whipped off her head and tumbled to the forest floor. Strands of hair drifted freely. Her body sailed between the trees. Her face was stone.

Miss Greyson was flying.

Leaves flittered down; sticks broke off and bounced through the tangled branches. Miss Greyson arced through the canopy, thirty feet in the air, smashing through brittle foliage. Then she descended, graceful as an acrobat. Her feet touched the earth, and she galloped forward, a perfect landing.

But she didn't stop. Her saunter accelerated into a charge. Abner didn't run. He couldn't think. He just stood there, helpless, as Miss Greyson rammed into him.

But she didn't knock him over. She *grappled* him—threw an arm around his neck, another under his axilla. He turned, trying to shake her off. But then his feet no longer felt the ground.

Miss Miss Greyson was picking him up. They were levitating, together. Abner watched the land fall away. He was five feet up, then ten feet—a slow and frightening ascent. Logs and mushrooms shrank away. Vertigo took hold. And then, Abner felt Miss Miss Greyson let go. Wind rushed past his ears.

Abner hit the ground, sideways. Pain pounded through his spine. He expelled hot breath into the dirt. He couldn't move; he tried to inhale, but his lungs refused. He lay there, gasping, motionless. His cheek pressed into moist loam.

He forced himself to roll over, but it was too late. He watched in horror as Miss Greyson launched upward, soaring straight into the treetops. High above, she was suspended for long seconds—then she fell again, straight down, into Abner's paralyzed body.

Her heavy wooden heels bashed Abner's side. He heard a rib crack. He tried to scream, but he had no breath. Miss Greyson straddled him, knees digging in. She didn't weigh a single pound, but her body still had mass, density. She was a battleship—hard and strong, yet buoyant.

She lifted off again, rising into the trees. And then, all at once, Abner realized what was happening.

She's trying to kill me. She won't stop until I'm dead.

Abner imagined himself dying this way—stomped again and again, until his bones were shattered, his chest crushed, his body mangled beyond recognition. Of all the demises he had ever feared, this was the worst: to be slowly beaten to death by an enemy he couldn't fight.

Abner roused himself. He heaved his body to the edge of a thick tree. He looked up, watching Miss Greyson's figure diminish into the upper branches. He lifted himself into a sitting position and huddled against the bark. He wrapped his arms around his throbbing torso, bracing himself for the next attack.

He heard the whoosh of wind; the thud of Miss Greyson's boots. He saw her, legs askew, fingers splayed against the ground, panting. She reared. In an instant, she would spring forward, wrestle Abner to the ground, throng him without mercy—

But then Abner saw something. Another figure. Elizabeth. She stepped from the garbled bushes. There was something in her hand. A rock.

She swung it down. It struck Miss Greyson's skull. A sickening thump. Her head jolted. Her body stiffened. Her lashes fluttered, and then her eyes rolled back. A red *Y* was cut into her temple. It spat blood down her cheek. Miss Greyson stumbled once, then slumped sideways. Her body shuddered, and finally went still.

❖

Dr. O'Malley peered into his mail slot, but it was empty. Still no envelope, as he had hoped.

The professor adjusted the shoulder strap of his satchel and climbed the long stairway to his apartment. Squeals and shouts issued from the quad, and he grinned at the thought of future surgeons tossing snowballs at each other. Dr. O'Malley passed a broad window and saw the snow pouring down, the frozen confetti of the year's first blizzard.

He unlocked the door to his apartment and pushed his back against it. He took one final look at the storm blustering outside. Then he noticed the pool of light in his study. He silently cursed himself for leaving his desk lamp on.

Then he saw her—Elizabeth, leaning against his bookshelf, arms crossed.

"*Jumping Jehosephat!*" cried Dr. O'Malley. His bag slid off his arm and hit the worn Persian carpet. When Elizabeth said nothing, he said, "How in blazes did you get in here?"

"You should brew some tea," Elizabeth said.

Dr. O'Malley looked baffled for only a moment. He slipped into his kitchen and lit the gas range. Flame crowned the base of his teakettle. For a bachelor, Dr. O'Malley's apartment was spacious, with its own living room, a study in the corner, a generous master bedroom, and a quaint kitchen. The washroom even had its own bathtub. Each room had its own radiator. The domicile warm, and he dragged the scarf from his neck and bundled it atop the icebox.

Elizabeth moved into the kitchen and leaned against the doorframe. Dr. O'Malley retreated to the back of the room and lifted himself onto the counter. His legs swayed beneath him.

"You likely have a lot of questions," said Dr. O'Malley. "Ask anything you—"

"Henrietta Greyson," interjected Elizabeth. She raised her hand and tallied on her fingers: "Chemist. Professor. And the murderer of three nuns. Correct?"

"Correct," said Dr. O'Malley.

"I took your word for it," said Elizabeth. "And I believe you. I think she killed them. Yet I had to wonder—why nuns? And why those particular nuns? Does she hate religion? Did she like that they were old, and couldn't run away? Maybe she liked that they were cloistered, they'd be slow to call the police. So many sadistic possibilities, don't you think?"

Dr. O'Malley winced. "Is that a question?"

"No," said Elizabeth. "Not yet. Because I want to guess. I think I've earned the right."

"Well, then," Dr. O'Malley said. "Go on."

"Miss Greyson was fiery," began Elizabeth. "We all saw that. She's the kind of spinster young men fawn over—smart, pretty, seems to have a wild streak. Maybe she was always that way. But she was careless. She met the wrong boy." Elizabeth cocked her head sideways. "Am I on the right track?"

"Go on," said Dr. O'Malley.

"She told me her father was a good man. She said we had that in common. But in her case, I think that meant her mother was the opposite. I think her mother was a harpy. And I'll bet when Mother Greyson learned her daughter was pregnant, she sent her away—to Saint Majella's Abbey in Podunk, Massachusetts."

Dr. O'Malley looked at the floor. "Nuns were never more cruel than to a fallen woman."

"I'm sure they were," Elizabeth spat. "Cruel, that is. We all know nuns treat those girls like slaves. But it was worse than that. Because after nine months, they took her child away." She glared at Dr. O'Malley. "Didn't they?"

The kettle whistled. Steam jetted into the air. Dr. O'Malley slid down from his roost and poured water into two cups.

"It was a wicked thing," he said, handing a cup to Elizabeth. "No girl should ever have to endure such a loss. And so, for Henrietta to seek revenge—I can't begrudge her that. The child is gone forever. Its name is lost. I can't believe she even saw the newborn's face before the Sisters stole it away. And if it were me, I might have killed the bitches myself."

Elizabeth glowered. "But that's not the reason."

"What reason? What do you mean?"

"The reason you never turned her in. You pitied her, I'm sure. But justice isn't what you're after. You want to know *her secret*."

Dr. O'Malley nodded serenely. "Quite so. Now—what did you find out?"

Elizabeth raised a finger. "Not so fast, professor. I want to know what's going on. Who *are* you? And what's your role in this?"

"Elizabeth—"

"I've stalked a murderer for three days. I have a right to know, haven't I?"

Dr. O'Malley sighed through his tapered nostrils. He bowed his head in silent acquiescence. Then he raised his fingers to the base of his throat. He grasped his bowtie and began to unravel it, then unfastened his top button. The gesture alarmed Elizabeth. She instinctively stepped back. But Dr. O'Malley only reached into his shirt, grasped something within, and drew it out.

A delicate silver chain spilled down his chest. At the bottom hung a small ring. The metal was dull gray, like unpolished pewter. He took the ring delicately in his fingertips and held it toward the light.

Elizabeth crept toward it, mouth agape. The ring was topped with a disc, and Elizabeth squinted at the tiny figure cut into its surface. In the center was a tree, and leaves radiated in different directions. Above it, a crescent curved sideways.

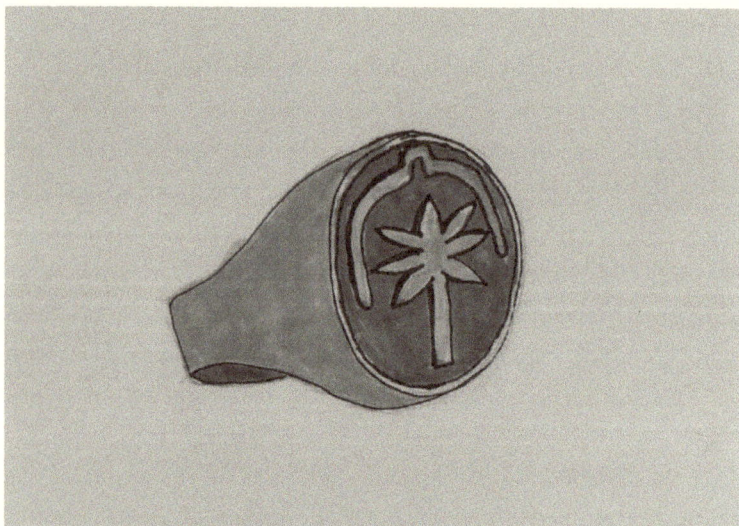

"What—what does it mean?"

"This," intoned Dr. O'Malley, "is my most prized possession. I wouldn't trade it for a heap of diamonds. It's just a piece of jewelry, mind you. But what it *means*—has shaped the story of my life. Without this ring, I'd still be a worthless bruiser, picking fights on Eden Quay."

"A secret society," whispered Elizabeth.

"Now, quid pro quo," said Dr. O'Malley, stuffing the ring back into his shirt. "What did you find?"

Elizabeth took a long breath. "I'm no chemist," said Elizabeth. "It's by far my weakest subject. But I think she was experimenting with helium."

"She was *what?*" Dr. O'Malley slammed down his teaset down his tea. He ripped slipped the glasses from his nose. "Helium, you say? To what end?"

"Helium is lighter than air," Elizabeth went on. "Every child with a rubber balloon knows that. And helium is a gas—unless it's minus 452 degrees Fahrenheit, which it never is, not even in Massachusetts."

"Certainly," agreed Dr. O'Malley. "Then what was she trying to do?"

"Miss Greyson has cannisters of the stuff in her own home," Elizabeth said slowly. "What if—you could extract the property of helium that gives it lift? Or you mixed helium with something else, to make it liquid? What if you could inject this serum into your veins? What if you could make your bloodstream *lighter than air?*"

"My God," breathed Dr. O'Malley. "She gave herself the ability to fly?"

"That was the idea. But I'm guessing she had to be careful. Too much of the serum, and she would float away. Not enough, and she'd never leave the ground. So she gave herself enough to leap great distances. Like a flying squirrel."

"Of course," marveled Dr. O'Malley. "That's how she assailed the abbey—she *flew*."

"Precisely. She snuck through the first sister's window. No need for doors. Then, later, she jumped over the garden wall. And finally, she used the window again to the Mother Superior's study. That's why there were only two footprints in the middle of the desk—she must have sprung across the entire room and landed there. Then she knocked the old woman down, dragged her across the room, and threw her out the window. Once the deed was done, she simply flew away before anyone could spot her."

"A shrewder plot was never hatched," seethed Dr. O'Malley.

"But I don't think she planned it that way," said Elizabeth. "I don't think Miss Greyson is a killer—not by nature. She's kind. She's mothering. And when they took away her child, she must have turned her attentions to science. She experimented in that cottage for a long time. Living in the woods gave her a private place to run her tests. She wanted a patent, not a weapon. She wanted to *discover* something." Elizabeth shook her head. "But then she saw she had a deadly instrument. The abbey was *so close*. The women who had stolen her child were still there, and no one would ever punish them for the things they did. She could finally have revenge. She could make them suffer, just as she had suffered. And no one would be the wiser."

"Incredible," said Dr. O'Malley, blinking aloofly. "But how do you know all this?"

"I went to her house."

"You did *what?*"

Elizabeth scrunched her face. "I went this afternoon. I knew her schedule, and I thought she would be in class all day." She rolled her head. "I took Abner."

"Abner *Cohen?*" burst Dr. O'Malley. "The Jew-boy on the basketball squad? Why the devil did you take *him?*"

"For starters, he's my only friend," rejoined Elizabeth. "And for your information, he probably saved my life. Miss Greyson came home early, and if Abner hadn't distracted her, I'd be buried in her backyard by now."

"Forgive me," said Dr. O'Malley. "He's a devoted friend, I can tell. No disrespect. But did she see his face?"

"She did more than that. She chased him into the woods. She beat him to a pulp. She broke two of his ribs and gave him a concussion. And she would have kept going. She would have killed him, if..."

"If what?"

Elizabeth hardened. She jutted her chin. "If I hadn't hit her with a rock."

Dr. O'Malley was aghast. His eyes popped. He grabbed his scarf and moved toward the doorway. "Where is she now?"

"She's *dead*, professor," Elizabeth said.

"Dead?"

"Yes. We dragged her to her house, and I put her inside." She paused. "And then I spread kerosene on the floor and set it on fire. So it would look like an accident."

Before Dr. O'Malley could grasp what she had said, Elizabeth reached into her pocket and drew a packet of papers. "But first I nabbed these. In case you want to learn how to fly."

Elizabeth tossed the packet on the counter. She re-folded her arms.

"I... I don't know what to say," Dr. O'Malley stammered. "You... *killed* her?"

"I don't think of myself a killer," said Elizabeth evenly. "All things being equal, I wouldn't hurt a butterfly. And Miss Greyson was good to me. She said kind things. But when she started hurting Abner—something changed in me, professor. I had to stop her, at any cost."

Dr. O'Malley studied Elizabeth. She was so young and gangly; a strong draft might knock her over. Yet her posture was bold. Her eyes burned. She looked as ironclad as anyone Dr. O'Malley had ever met. He saw the passion in her face, the hunger, the resolution. Elizabeth Crowne was everything he had hoped for.

"I think I've paid my dues, professor," said Elizabeth.

"I should say you have," agreed Dr. O'Malley. "Now we've reached a fork in the road. I won't blame you for staying here, if that's your choice."

"We both know that's not my choice," Elizabeth rebutted.

"Very well, then." Dr. O'Malley opened the kettle and dumped the remaining water into the sink. It splashed over white porcelain and gurgled down the drain. "You'd better pack your things. We leave in the morning."

"Leave? For where?"

"For London, my dear. And write your folks. We'll be away for quite some time."

First Letter

November, 1912

Dear Ab,

Not that it matters, but I am writing you from a hotel in
Boston. My room is dark and freezing, and although the
window is sealed, everything smells of cigarettes and fish. My
view is high enough to see the shipping cranes, and if the sky
weren't so dense with clouds, I could watch the sun setting
beyond the warehouse rooftops. I suppose this is as romantic
as a harbor flophouse gets.

All right, here's the solemn truth: I'm sorry I left you at
Saint Luke's. I'm sorry I abandoned you in that infirmary,
banged up and unconscious. I'm sorry you woke up alone,
wondering where I went. I'm sorry you're receiving this letter
so many days later, convinced that I've left you for good. You
were thoroughly trounced, and all on my behalf. My only
consolation is that a medical school is probably the best place
to get patched up; you can't throw a stethoscope without
hitting a future surgeon.

I'm also thankful—thankful beyond words. You probably saved my life, and I'll never forget it. I'd like to think we're even, but if you hadn't distracted Miss Greyson, I wouldn't have been around to save your life. You are a brave fellow, Abner, despite your fear of small spaces. You're also the first man to ever steer me away from death. Not bad for a junior.

You're also the only person I trust, perhaps in the whole world. Sneer not at this distinction. I don't even trust the *word* trust, so consider yourself the club's only member. Now I need a confidante, so do me a favor and accept this burden. Normally I keep my secrets close, but recent events have pushed me to the brink. If I don't spill the beans, I'll explode. So please, *please* keep the contents of this missive private.

Here goes: I've run away with Professor O'Malley.

Now don't panic. We're not eloping. Quite the opposite: I think O'Malley is some sort of secret agent. Not some dime-novel spy, but the genuine article. And if that doesn't astonish you, how about this: O'Malley invited me to travel with him to London. Which is precisely what I'm doing.

Why should I do such a thing? Drop out of school, skip town, leave my family indefinitely? Am I just foolish girl, led astray by a mad professor? If only it were that simple.

All this time has passed, Abner, and I feel I've told you nothing. That's always been my way, I suppose. I spent the first twenty-one years of my life reading dense books in private. In my heyday, I doubt there was a bookworm in Pittsburgh less social than I. The closest thing I had to a playmate was my grandfather's chess set. If I'd worn more ribbons, I might have made some lady friends, and if I didn't love climbing trees, the boys might've looked my way. A gal with skinned knees and a talent for Latin tends to go it alone.

My insect collection probably didn't help—nothing unnerves people more than pins and beetles.

Here is a fact I have kept hidden, even from you: My father is a brilliant academic. Breathe the name "Dr. Benedict Crowne" in the echoing halls of the Ivy League, and grown men will swoon with admiration. Among the most learned northeastern scholars, he is a toasted celebrity, and every dean in the country would fall over himself to host one of my father's lectures. To describe his work requires some time, because his specialty is a confounding cross-section of biology, linguistics, and higher maths. His papers are incomprehensible to the common man, and even their abstracts run for pages.

Yet to me, Dr. Crowne is merely "Dad," a clumsy man with a nerve-wracking stutter. Alone, he can neither tie a tie nor find a matching cardigan. He has wandered out of the house without shoes, traversing snow banks in his socks. He is late for everything, forgets all appointments, and can barely read his own chicken scratch. His desk is crowded with teacups, each vessel half-full of cloudy sludge. Three times a year, my father has another chance to remember a child's birthday, and every time he fails to muster even a card. He meanders through a haze of hypotheses, oblivious to the tactile world. I don't begrudge my father his intellect, but geniuses are a clumsy bunch. He spills the contents of his briefcase at least once a day, and no toe is left unstubbed. If I had a nickel for every time Dr. Crowne forgot his bifocals somewhere, I could hire him a full-time optometrist.

I never doubt my father's good intentions, which is more than most daughters can say. Buried inside all that gray matter, my father loves me. In my early girlhood, he always tucked me in. Each Noël, he gathered my brother and sister and me around the hearth and read *'Twas the Night Before Christmas*. Most vitally, if I asked a question, no matter how misguided, my father always took the time to answer in full. He has a talent for oration, and by golly, that man can ruminate.

If the apple never falls far from the tree, I sometimes think I'm two different apples. I have always been bright, like him. I have always locked myself in a study, like him. I have always believed in the providential power of science, like him. I could pretend that I am only one apple, the one that fell close. I could stagger in his footsteps, become a respectable biologist or physician, or mix vials all day in the cozy isolation of a lab. I could patch up cuts and send happy new mothers on their way.

But then there's the other apple, the one that fell far. The apple that's proudly misshapen. The apple that rolled down the hill and got swept down a stream and ended up God-knows-where. The apple that no one will toss in a basket or bake in a pie. Some call this the "bad apple." But frankly, I like them apples.

You know me as well as anyone, Abner—which is absurd, because it means there's not much to know. I've done little with my twenty-one years on Earth, just bumbled about libraries and aced a few exams. But I'm a daredevil at heart. You might not think it. "What bird-watcher loves risk?" you might wonder.

But for years, I would hike into a narrow valley near my family house, a hidden place called Junction Hollow. I would walk along the railroad bed, squeezed between wooded hills. The hollow lies in the middle of the city, yet I felt far from anything, a Crusoe on my private island. It was there that I watched trains roll past. I could stand within spitting distance of a locomotive and its queue of creaking boxcars. I poked around the undersides of bridges, their stone piers rising like towers above me. I flipped over stones to see earthworms and scattering ants. I spent entire days in that empty park, studying the piles of railroad ties, the moist stumps of trees overflowing with life, the brick walls covered in the graffiti of bygone tramps. Never had I felt such joy.

If someone had tapped me on the shoulder and invited me to ride a camel across the Sahel, I would have done it. Scour the bottom of the sea in a rusty diving bell? Yes. Summit Andean mountains with a flea-bitten llama? I wouldn't think twice. No one knows how many *National Geographics* I stuffed under my mattress and read by candlelight at forbidden hours. My encyclopedia is dog-eared with thumbing. The hours I've spent daydreaming of adventure outnumber the hours I've spent on my feet, a ratio I plan to invert. I swear, Abner, one day I'll fly in an aeroplane. I'll sip coffee with dervishes and fly kites in Peking. Just you wait.

I fear no one will understand my rambling, but you have always listened, and no one deserves an explanation more. I am ready for my life to truly begin. I may be slight, but one day I hope to cast a long shadow.

Your Friend,

Liz

THE PALACE OF
WAYWARD DREAMS

December, 1912

C HECK," declared Sir Shanley.
In one swipe, his white knight clacked against the marble chess board, and he plucked up a black pawn. He leaned into the cushions of his rattan chair and held up the captured piece.

Larimer growled at this. His paws met in front of his chin, and he examined the grid with aquamarine eyes. The game had started evenly, but Sir Shanley was hastening his assault. Essential pieces were gathered on the edges of the board—including Larimer's queen.

"You know, old boy," said Sir Shanley, laying down the pawn with exaggerated flourish. "I wouldn't be averse to starting over."

"My bishop," purred Larimer. "That was my mistake."

"You mean you advanced too soon," said Sir Shanley, rubbing his cheek. "I would tend to agree. But there's no shame in surrender. I'm rather weary of all this *thinking*, anyhow. Mightn't we get back to pachisi? Much simpler, wouldn't you agree?"

Larimer scanned the long marble table, which was etched with the patterns of other board games—the lines and circles of pachisi, the indents of Chinese checkers, the concentric squares of Nine Men's Morris, the craters of Mancala, and the narrow triangles of backgammon. Beyond lay several packs of shuffled cards and the piled tiles of mahjong. Larimer shielded his eyes; as always, the orange sun bled drowsily through a latticed bamboo screen. A fan spun slowly above them, its shadow circling the table.

"I don't care," said Larimer, his tail swishing the floor. "They're all insipid to me."

"Insipid," echoed Sir Shanley. He gathered the chess pieces into a pile. "You just need practice."

The whish of sandals roused Sir Shanley from his stupor. He squinted his aged eyes, and the long hall came into focus: The scrawny figure of Maung scampered down the stone floor. He was a stick figure of a boy, his knees knocking awkwardly inside his colorful *longyi*. He reached the table, doubled over, and held his heaving chest. Sir Shanley grinned, bemused by the child's exaggerated panting.

"Welcome, m'lad," he said. "What's the news?"

"Miss… Miss…" Maung straightened out. "Miss Maybell is here to see you."

Sir Shanley rose to his feet. Maung looked over his shoulder, and they both watched a woman approach. *Miss Maybell*. She sauntered down the imperious hall in a pearly tea dress. Her dark curls were pinned up, but several locks hung free along her rouged face. She cooled herself furiously with a red fan. Maung kowtowed and backed away from the arriving lady.

"Miss Maybell," intoned Sir Shanley.

"Sir Shanley," she said. She curtseyed curtly. "I trust you're well."

"Right as rain. And you?"

"I'm—well. Thank you."

For a long moment, Miss Maybell's eyes drifted. They fell, as always, upon Larimer. She could not hide her disdain; her lips and eyebrows crumpled, as if she had swallowed a lemon. Larimer looked away, avoiding her eyes—but his twitching feline ears betrayed a mutual discomfort. The silence built. Sir Shanley felt himself redden.

"Might I have a word?" asked Miss Maybell.

Sir Shanley looked at Larimer. "With your permission?"

"Of course, of *course*," exclaimed Larimer, waving a paw in the air. Sir Shanley could tell that Larimer was annoyed— claws peeked out of his knuckles' fur.

Sir Shanley moved away from the table; Miss Maybell followed. They found an arbitrary spot, a safe distance from Larimer and Maung. They leaned in close; Sir Shanley whiffed her jasmine perfume. She was perhaps thirty years old, only half his age. Still, he stole a glance at her elfin ears, the ceramic curve of her neck.

"I'm going back," said Miss Maybell.

"Going back?" exclaimed Sir Shanley. "But why?"

"I feel I've…" She hesitated. "I've had *enough*."

"Come, come," said Sir Shanley. He took her hand and pressed it. "These feelings—they happen to the best of us. There's no reason to fret. We've all the time in the world."

But Miss Maybell looked distracted. Sir Shanley followed her gaze back to the table, where Larimer was seated. An ugly feeling flooded him. But what was it? Shame? Embarrassment? Yet why should he feel that way? He knew that Miss Maybell disliked being around Larimer. But *was* it dislike, or mere anxiety? The latter he could understand— Larimer's presence was always alarming, at first. But wasn't it unfair? He had never been unkind to her. He had always played the proper gentleman.

Yes, there was Larimer's appearance. But the others never judged him for it. They treated him equitably, as if he were one of them. It was only Miss Maybell who shied away from him. Their conversations were brief and blunt. Predictably, Larimer avoided her as well. It was all so *frustrating*. Everyone else got on just fine. If she could only see past—

"How long have you been here?" Miss Maybell said sharply.

"I'm sorry?"

"I know what you've told people. Three or four days, is it?"

"Oh—you mean *real* days?"

"Yes. How long?"

"Oh, it's hard to say. Time works differently, here, as you know—"

"Longer than the others, I gather."

"Quite so."

"*Far* longer, I'd wager."

"What's all this?" Sir Shanley willed himself to show surprise. "Is something amiss?"

"What I mean is," Miss Maybell returned, "no one remembers you coming here. When they arrived, you were already here."

"Tosh!" said Sir Shanley, forcing a laugh. "You must be mistaken. What about Vikram? He's been here much longer than I have, I'm sure of it."

"He hasn't. I asked him."

"Well, how would anyone know, anyhow?" coaxed Sir Shanley. "It's not as if they hang calendars around here."

"You mean *we* don't hang calendars," corrected Miss Maybell. "It's *our* choice what gets hung and what doesn't. *We* decide everything that happens here, don't we? And I've a suspicion you prefer it that way."

He shrugged. "Don't we all?"

"Not me. No longer."

Sir Shanley wanted to protest. But what good would it do? He had watched so many others leave. How many? Dozens? Scores? But he decided to swallow his disappointment. She couldn't stay forever. No one ever did.

"Well, I shall miss you, Miss Maybell," he said, puffing his chest.

"You don't *have* to, you know."

She looked at him suggestively. Her small irises trembled in place. She was asking, now. It sickened him. He wanted to turn away. Or perhaps he wanted to explain. But he must keep feigning ignorance. He mustn't give in. He *couldn't* give in. Painful as it was, he would have to cut her loose.

"I'm grateful for the time we've had," he said. "And you are always welcome back."

Miss Maybell grimaced at this. She stepped away.

"Very well, then," she murmured. "Goodbye, Theodore. We'll always have—wherever this is."

For an instant, Sir Shanley felt a pang of regret— something he hadn't felt for a long, long time. He watched Miss Maybell walk away, into the blinding sun. The golden sphere burned around her, a corona of solar light, until her form lost its edges. She was only a dark daub in its center. And then, soundlessly, Miss Maybell vanished from sight.

❖

"I trust you won't mind an Irish breakfast," said Dr. O'Malley as he set down two coffee cups on the table. The saucers juddered, and concentric circles rippled on the surface of the aromatic liquid.

Elizabeth closed her magazine and frowned. "What makes it Irish?"

O'Malley pulled back his tweed jacket, revealing a leather holster. But instead of a weapon, he drew a prim green bottle, uncorked it, and poured generously into his own cup. He gave Elizabeth's coffee a splash as well.

"Not exactly Earl Gray, is it?" said Elizabeth, feeling the whiskey singe her throat.

"I take my sabbaticals seriously," said Dr. O'Malley. "And in future, I hope you'll toast me *before* sipping."

"Oh, right."

They clinked cups and drank. Elizabeth peered over the porcelain rim to admire the scenery: Through the dining car window, she watched the dark English countryside speed past—the subtle roll of the horizon, the mossy green of its scrub, and the sheets of mist that swallowed distant cottages. Stately stone walls crisscrossed the land, and herds of sheep crept across mown meadows.

As the train trundled down the track, and the dining car creaked and vibrated, Elizabeth felt ever more elated. She had always loved trains. Back in Pittsburgh, she had risen each morning to a whistle blowing in the hollow near her house. She even loved climbing aboard the Pittsburgh trolley, its crush of passengers, the flashes of buildings between the metal bars, the stop-go movement at every intersection. Even now she marveled at the bow-tied waiters darting about the dining car with platters of fried eggs and sausage. She marveled at how easily they moved across the rocking floor.

Dr. O'Malley unveiled his pipe and drew on it contemplatively. He seemed lost in thought. The usual silence.

Yet Elizabeth was compelled to break it. "So, tell me about this *Sir Shanley*."

Dr. O'Malley's head snapped up. A gust of smoke burst from his nostrils.

"Come again?"

"Sir Shanley, the man we're meeting in Nestershire."

"I—" Dr. O'Malley furrowed his brow. "How—?"

"Well, *obviously*," said Elizabeth, rolling her eyes, "I looked through your letters. Which is really your own fault, because you left the flap of your satchel open *at least* a dozen times. In my book, that's a formal invitation to eavesdrop."

"You—read my correspondence?"

"Of course. But don't worry—his handwriting is atrocious. I could barely read a word. And I clearly only had *his* letters to *you*."

Dr. O'Malley glowered through the smoke. "Elizabeth, if we are to work together, I will need your trust. This is... well, it's an invasion of privacy."

"Oh, don't be so dramatic," scoffed Elizabeth. She bent a knee in the booth to retie her boot. "Anyway, we've crossed an ocean together, and you haven't offered so much as a peep about this *secret society*—"

"*Ssh!*" Dr. O'Malley scanned the car.

"Professor," said Elizabeth, "who here could possibly care? And I'll remind you that half of the phrase 'secret society' is *society*. I'm not feeling like much of a member."

Dr. O'Malley sank into his seat. "Elizabeth, you mustn't be so flip. We are here on serious business—"

"Oh, *are* we?" retorted Elizabeth. "Then maybe I should know something about it."

"Elizabeth…" Dr. O'Malley bit his upper lip. "I know the journey's been long. But I promise—all will be revealed when we arrive in Nestershire."

Elizabeth spread her arms across the bench. "You're confused," she said. "I *adore* long journeys. We could take a steamer to Siam, for all I care. But at the end of fifteen days, I get to wondering *why*."

Dr. O'Malley flipped open his pocket watch. "In an hour and a half, you'll learn everything you yearn to know. Until then, you might shush about the *ecretsay ocietysay*."

Elizabeth smiled gaily. "Tell me your secret code is actually Pig Latin."

Dr. O'Malley cracked a smile as he pocketed his watch. "Wouldn't you like to know?"

They both grinned and drained the last of their cups.

❖

Passengers trickled out of the train. Elizabeth took a breath of damp air and lugged her bags onto the station platform. Nearby, the locomotive hissed jets of steam, which overlapped with the sounds of reuniting families. Travelers embraced their loved ones, shook hands with friends, lifted children into their arms. Elizabeth weaved between bunches of people. She passed the station house and its uniformed attendants, then found herself on a quiet avenue.

Dr. O'Malley scrambled to catch up, thanks to his two enormous suitcases. Elizabeth was tickled to know that she packed lighter than her professor—until she'd learned that the bulk of his luggage was books, which made her envious.

"I assume you know the way," said Elizabeth.

"I do," replied Dr. O'Malley. "Towns like Nestershire don't change much."

Ranks of brick houses stood at attention, and their narrow roofs sloped into each other, endless chevrons of slate. Dense floral curtains clogged the rectangular windows, and cold weather had colored the low hedges a dull brown. But Elizabeth adored the red doorways, the crenellations and ornate bargeboards, the efflorescence that stained the chimneys white, the jetties that loomed over the narrow streets. Each home fit snugly against its neighbors, as quaint and refined as dollhouses.

Skinny as she was, Elizabeth enjoyed the chill as well, and the brooding overcast agreed with her. She had never minded the long Pittsburgh winter, with its hazy darkness and sheets of freezing rain, and England seemed to share its cheerless climate. They crossed a plaza ringed with shops, empty except for a lone delivery man and his wagon.

"The hotel's still there," Dr. O'Malley noted aloud.

"Are we staying there?" Elizabeth asked.

"Not if we can help it. But it all depends."

"Depends on what?"

"On whether anyone's at home."

Bells rang from a nearby steeple. Elizabeth had no watch, and when she counted ten clangs of the bell, she marveled at how early it still was. She felt drowsy but excited, and she was too lost in thought to realize she was walking alone.

"Elizabeth!" Dr. O'Malley called.

She turned around and saw the professor standing on the curb, nearly a block behind her.

"It's this one!" he announced.

Like the others, this house was tucked into the row of façades, and Elizabeth would never have given the building a second glance. But now that Dr. O'Malley had pointed it out, Elizabeth smiled at its stately grandeur. Set back from the street, the domicile was more like a small mansion, with manicured bushes and mullioned windows. The doorway was a masterpiece of wood and glass, and the lead framework was shaped into swirls and curlicues. The double doors reminded Elizabeth of a cathedral.

They crossed the stone walkway, thick with fallen leaves. Dr. O'Malley gripped the brass knocker and tapped it against its plate.

The door opened. A trim woman stood before them, wiping her hands on her apron. Her wavy blonde hair flared out beneath her maid's bonnet. Elizabeth was startled: Despite her stodgy uniform, the girl was disarmingly pretty. Her mouth was small and serious, and her eyes were skeptically narrow.

"I…" Dr. O'Malley fumbled. "That is…"

"We're here to see Mr. Shanley," interrupted Elizabeth.

"*Sir* Shanley," corrected Dr. O'Malley. "That is—we're here to see *Teddy*, miss. I'm an old friend. Is he in?"

"I…"

The girl looked sideways. Something was amiss.

"At least," said Elizabeth, "could we come in? It's not exactly warm out here."

The maid bit her lip. At last, she nodded and ushered them inside. They followed her through the vestibule and into a sitting room. The bookshelves and furniture were all chestnut brown, a patchwork of wood and leather. Right in the middle, there was a table, and in the middle of the table, an island of mail. The white envelopes were all unopened, the same addresses written over and over in the same hand.

"Please," said the maid, "just wait right here."

"Yes," stuttered Dr. O'Malley. "Of course. Certainly." As the maid shuffled out of the room, the professor couldn't help but follow her with his eyes.

They set down their bags and slumped into opposite chairs. Elizabeth removed her gloves and rubbed her hands together. She gestured to the pile of untouched mail. "I suppose this explains why he never wrote you back."

Dr. O'Malley clucked his tongue thoughtfully. "So—you read *all* the letters?"

"All the letters you had on you. But we both know he stopped sending them about six weeks ago."

Now that they were seated, Elizabeth felt road-weary, and she sank into the plush upholstery. She could feel the heaviness, the ache in her shoulders. But then, surprisingly, she giggled.

"Something funny?" asked Dr. O'Malley.

"All this time together," said Elizabeth, "and I still introduce you as *Professor O'Malley*."

Dr. O'Malley smirked. "Would you prefer to use my Christian name?"

"I don't even know your Christian name," Elizabeth teased. "Anyway, I can respect a professional distance. And I wouldn't want to give your new *sweetheart* the wrong idea." Elizabeth jutted her chin toward the entrance, where the maid had just departed.

Dr. O'Malley sniffed at this. He patted his knee with rhythmic impatience. "*My new sweetheart.* I should be so lucky."

Silence followed. One minute, followed by another. Elizabeth didn't like it. They were *here*, at last, after so many days at sea. But what was supposed to happen *now?* They had weathered ports and gangplanks and two storms. They'd shared a cabin, slept in opposite bunks, and traded shifts in the lavatory. They had eaten meals together, wandered the decks, drank coffee and tea, and watched sunrises and sunsets. Yet through it all, Elizabeth had learned little about her mentor. Dr. O'Malley was an exuberant teacher; why so quiet on the road? Dr. O'Malley had passed entire afternoons reclined on his mattress, one arm resting on his forehead as the other held an open book. So little had been explained. And now?

Before Elizabeth could think of something else to say, the maid stepped back into the room. She spoke directly to the carpet.

"Lady Shanley will see you now."

❖

Elizabeth had never seen a hearth so large. Dark stone and mortar ringed the vast opening; Elizabeth could have stood inside the fireplace and barely needed to tilt her head. Behind a black grille, massive logs crackled with flame. A Persian carpet was sprawled on floorboards as thick as railroad ties.

The ceiling was high and vaulted; the wood beams radiated from a central point. Even the fire pokers looked outsized, like medieval weapons hanging from the wall.

"Mum," murmured the maid from the doorway. "Your guests are here. Mr. O'Malley and Miss Crowne."

From the edge of the chamber, Lady Shanley was hidden in her high-backed chair. Elizabeth waited for a response, but there was nothing. She mustered her courage and ventured into the den, followed by Dr. O'Malley. They rounded the carpet, and the woman emerged behind the upholstery. Lady Shanley was brittle and pale; her lips had turned violet. Her skin barely seemed to stretch over her tiny head. Two wizened fingers were splayed across her chapped lips. A ring of embroidery lay on her lap, where she had threaded a few meaningless shapes. Yet, she was a noble presence; her hair retained its auburn hue, and she wore a flattering wool gown. The woman was not old enough for wrinkles or spots, and she retained the handsomeness of middle age. Lady Shanley gazed into the glowing hearth, unmoved by her new company.

Elizabeth curtseyed—clumsily—in the flickering light. For an instant, the woman seemed to break from her trance.

"Lady Shanley," Elizabeth murmured. "How do you do?"

"I'm lovely, dear, thank you," the woman responded. She smiled vacantly, as if she had no idea what she was smiling about. She affixed a thimble and went back to her needlework, drawing colored thread through the blank fabric. Elizabeth lingered there a moment, hoping the woman would ask a question, but the only sound was the crackle of the fire.

Elizabeth looked at Dr. O'Malley helplessly, but her professor only shook his head in dismay. In tandem, they backed away from the scene, tiptoeing to the corridor. The maid hadn't moved from the doorframe; she took one final glance into the room, made sure Lady Shanley was consumed in her stitches, and pushed the heavy door shut.

"Forgive me, miss," whispered Dr. O'Malley, "but what in blazes is going on here?"

"*Not here,*" the maid whispered back. She crooked a finger, ushering them forward. They followed her down a staircase, slipped through a doorway, into a little courtyard.

December was a dreary time of year, and the small space looked colorless and damp. The court was paved with cobblestone, and a handful of clay pots were full of dry soil and dead plants. Two stone benches stood on either end of the court, and all around them rose half-timbered walls and dark windows.

The maid drew a metal case from her apron pocket and placed a cigarette between her lips. Dr. O'Malley rushed to her with a packet of matches, and soon the girl was inhaling deeply, her eyes distant.

"What's your name, anyhow?" asked Elizabeth.

"Alexandra," she answered. "But Lexi, really."

"Listen, Lexi, I know we're strangers, but we're here to help. At least…" Elizabeth shot a glance at Dr. O'Malley. "I'm *assuming* that's why we're here."

"I guessed as much," said Lexi, waving smoke away. "And that's precisely why I showed you Lady Shanley just now. She's gone daft, as you can tell. She speaks nary a word."

"But Lexi," Dr. O'Malley said gently, "where is Teddy? If not here, then where has he gone?"

"Down the way," said Lexi. "To the other side of town."

"So you know where he is?"

"Ay," said Lexi. "But I fear what's happened to him. You see, I think we've lost him."

"How do you mean? Lost him, how?"

Lexi swallowed. "To opium."

❖

Lexi's voice was soft and warbled. She never looked them in the eye. She burned each cigarette to the nub, pausing only to light a fresh one. Dr. O'Malley bade her sit down, but the girl stayed on her feet.

"It seemed like such a normal place," Lexi began. "When Sir Shanley hired me on, I was so grateful, sir, I truly was. This house—I had never seen its like. It was so grand, so beautiful. And the master was so kind. The missus, too. I never knew service could be so sublime. I swore I'd do anything to keep this job, no matter what they asked."

Yet the job was strange, she said. There was no butler, no valet, and Lexi herself was the only full-time maid. They employed one cook, who still prepared their meals, but she drifted in and out of the kitchen, without assistants or fanfare. Every few months, some workers arrived—to clean the gutters, sweep the chimney, or repair some old brickwork. But that was all. Otherwise, the house was quiet. Lexi fancied her job—it wasn't easy, given the endless rooms to dust and arrange, but it wasn't difficult, either. The Shanleys were a tranquil couple. There were no ashtrays to clear, no guests to serve, no elaborate meals to clean up. Sir Shanley roamed from room to room, occupying himself with a book or newspaper. He wrote long letters in his study. His wife was pleasant enough, but her only real pastime was her embroidery. They barely spoke, and the house could fall silent for days. Visitors were rare. Lexi wondered what she should do if anyone knocked.

Ever the dutiful maid, Lexi finished her tasks quickly, but this left many idle hours. Sometimes, to occupy her time, she borrowed books from Sir Shanley's study.

"I had permission, though!" she interjected. "To look at the books, I mean. The master said as much. I could take any book I liked, so long as I returned it to the proper spot."

Elizabeth was startled by the maid's defensiveness. "Anything good in there?" she simpered.

Lexi blushed. "Honestly, I'm not well schooled. And I reckon most of them books aren't even English. But I fancy the pictures, you see."

"But there were no *signs*," Dr. O'Malley pressed. "Of distress or despair?"

"Not at first," said Lexi. "But then, one evening, Master Shanley went out."

"Was there anything strange about his behavior?"

"Well," said Lexi, "mostly that he went out at all. I'd hardly ever seen the man out-of-doors."

Sir Shanley had seemed excited about something. He gave a flurry of instructions—*turn down the bed, keep the fire going*—chores Lexi planned to do anyway. Sir Shanley quickly threw on his own coat, before Lexi had a chance to help him. Then he flew into the street, leaving the front door ajar.

"If I didn't know better, I'd say he looked nervous," Lexi said. "Not frightened. Only—like I said, nervous."

Lexi was flummoxed. Where was her master going? To the pub? Surely not. To a friend's house? What friends did he have, all of a sudden? It occurred to Lexi how little she knew about the man. Their home was like a museum, stately and impersonal. Its artifacts revealed little about her employers—

who they were, where they had been. They might as well be tenants in a stranger's house.

Sir Shanley returned around midnight. Lexi heard movement in the vestibule. She rushed to attend, but the old man had already started to ascend the staircase. She called his name, but Sir Shanley waved her away. He disappeared into the hall and slipped into his bedroom.

"And he never said where he went?" Dr. O'Malley inquired.

"Not a peep," answered Lexi. "Nor any of the other times."

"You mean it happened again?"

"Oh, yes. Many times. Twice a week, at least. For *months*. And each time he seemed more restless. I had never seen him like that before."

Sir Shanley never announced his departure. He dressed himself in private. He moved discreetly through the house. He left through different doors, escaping silently to the street. Sometimes hours would pass before Lexi was certain Sir Shanley was gone. He always came back, but his reappearances grew later and later—two in the morning, four. After a few weeks, Lexi no longer bothered to wait for him. Whatever he was up to, Sir Shanley was avoiding her.

But as his absences lengthened, Lexi became frightened for his welfare. What if Sir Shanley failed to come back at all? What should she do? Lexi had never interacted with police; truth be told, she had always been watchful of bobbies. She wanted to consult Lady Shanley, yet the woman showed little sign of concern. She spent her days migrating through the house, saying almost nothing. When the Cheshire cat occasionally emerged, Lady Shanley would stroke him for hours. She would stare through windows and watch birds build a nest in the neighbors' rooftop. She seemed unaware of anything awry.

Lexi found no comfort in her routine. She made the usual rounds; she shoveled ashes, polished silver, swept particles from the floors. But she couldn't lose herself in work, as she'd always done. Nor could she eat a full meal or sleep through the night. Without Sir Shanley in the house, the place felt hollow.

"Sometimes it was so quiet and empty, I wanted to scream," Lexi confessed. "And I was so worried for Master Shanley, I truly was."

"No doubt," sneered Elizabeth. "If anything happened to him, you'd have to hit the bricks."

"*Elizabeth*," shot Dr. O'Malley.

"It's true, though," Lexi said. "I *was* afraid. I owed them everything, and I feared what he was up to. But I also wondered—if the master was in trouble, what would happen to Lady Shanley? Or to me? I have cousins who were cast out on the street, and it's a horrid way to go. And if he were tangled in the wrong web, and if there was something I could do to prevent his ruin, how could I live with myself if I didn't try?"

"You followed him," Dr. O'Malley concluded. "Is that what you're saying?"

"I did," Lexi affirmed. "But you must know, it was only because I couldn't stand it any longer—"

"You were right to do so," Dr. O'Malley assured her. "But tell us, then—where did he go?"

"I followed him down the street," said Lexi. "It was difficult, because there was hardly anyone about, and if he heard any footsteps at all, he'd turn around and spot me. I had to keep my distance. Sometimes he was so far down the way, I thought I'd lose him. He walked for more than a mile, I reckon, clear across town. I don't mind saying, it's not the nicest street, the one he came to. There's a fair number of pubs, and a house of ill repute, I know that much. I nearly turned round—it's one thing to wander about such streets alone, but it's quite another to be *seen* there. A girl can get a reputation."

"Was it Lilac Way?" Dr. O'Malley asked.

"Ay, it was. Do you know it?"

"I do. And that, I presume, is where you found the opium den," said Dr. O'Malley.

"Yes, sir. And I can't say what came over me, but..." Lexi took a long breath. "I watched him go inside. And not long after, five minutes or thereabout, I crossed the street and knocked on that door myself. I've never been scared-er in my life, but I stood strong, I did. When a man cracked open the door, I said, 'The master of my house just came in here.' I said, 'I want to see the proprietor of this place. I have a message for him.' And just like that, the proprietor appeared. I hardly had to wait at all. He was a Chinaman. Not very old. Quite dignified, if I say so myself. He said, 'May I help you?' Just like that. He was well spoken. Gentleman-like."

"And what did you reply?"

"I said, 'The master of my house just stepped in, and he forgot his pocket watch.'"

"His pocket watch?"

"I took it," said Lexi. "From his coat pocket, that afternoon. I knew he wouldn't check for it, not till later. At first, I wanted him to think it was pilfered. That watch was special, I knew, and he would try to retrace his steps, maybe come home early. But when I saw him go inside that den, I felt a bit angry. I know it's not my place—but how *dare* he?

Sneak out, like a thief in the night? Abandon his wife, who's never done him wrong? How could he spend his time like that, puffing a pipe like a common vagabond? I wanted him to know I'd seen him. I wanted him to reconsider. Whatever his trouble, I wanted him to overcome it."

"When did all this take place?"

Lexi closed her eyes and swallowed hard. "Three weeks ago. If he's been home, I've not seen him."

"Three *weeks!*" Dr. O'Malley exclaimed.

"And…" Lexi pressed a hand against her cheek. "I fear that *I'm* the one who's made it worse. Handing them that pocket watch, like I did—could that have been the final straw? Was it the shame of being found out? Could *I* have—"

"Not at all," said Dr. O'Malley. "Whatever Sir Shanley has done, he's done of his own volition. You're as blameless as can be, and I'll hear no more speculation. But tell me this— would you recognize the place? The opium den?"

"I know exactly where it is. But I won't go there alone."

"We'll go together," Dr. O'Malley said. "We'll keep you safe, I promise."

Lexi threw her final cigarette to the ground and crushed it into the stones. "Well, let's go, then."

"Well," Dr. O'Malley said, "not *yet*. Miss Crowne and I have just arrived, and we ought to rest a few hours. We mustn't barrel into an opium den half-cocked."

"Ay," Lexi said, nodding abashedly. "Of course."

"Now, Lexi," Dr. O'Malley went on, "what you've said is most helpful to us, and I'm grateful. I hope you'll grant us a moment."

"Yes, certainly." Lexi straightened her apron and backed away, toward the door. "I'll prepare your rooms."

"We'd be much obliged," said Dr. O'Malley. He smiled tiredly. He pressed a fist to his lips, waiting for Lexi to shut the door.

Elizabeth sensed his whirling thoughts. She drifted to the bench and seated herself. She straightened her skirt, looked at the professor, and waited.

"All right," he said, crossing his arms. "You've been more than patient, Elizabeth. And you deserve an explanation."

After a long pause, Elizabeth said, "I hope you're not waiting for me to disagree."

Dr. O'Malley smirked, but the levity melted from his face. He seemed uncertain where to begin. "The man we are to meet," he said, "was a colonel in the British army. He was also a civil servant for some while. *And* he's a respected scholar. For many years, I was his apprentice." Dr. O'Malley wiggled his jaw from side to side. "Well, first I was his *clerk*. I was very young—younger than you, in fact. I helped with menial tasks. Kept his books. Organized his papers. What he saw in me, I'll never know. I was a foolish boy, a ne'er-do-well. He took a great risk, hiring a scrappy Dubliner. But each evening, when the work was done, he'd pour two tumblers of brandy, and he'd ask me questions." Dr. O'Malley shook his head wistfully. "Sir Shanley is the wisest man I ever met. Those conversations we held, in the light of the fireplace, shaped me into the man I am."

"He was like a father," said Elizabeth.

"But more than that," said Dr. O'Malley, "he was a *teacher*. And what I am about to tell you must never leave this yard. We shall only speak of it in private, and only when I say the coast is clear. For sixteen generations, we have kept our secret, and it is imperative—now more than ever—that our world remain clandestine. Do you swear to protect this secret? Do you swear to take it to your deathbed?"

No one had ever spoken to Elizabeth in this way. The severity of Dr. O'Malley's words was etched in his expression. Gravely she replied, "Yes. I promise."

Dr. O'Malley stepped close to Elizabeth. He turned his chin downward; he seemed to speak into his own lapels.

"We are a secret order of scholars and investigators," he whispered. "Our purpose is to study *the uncanny*. As you have witnessed, the world is full of strange events—and most of us would choose not to believe them. We ignore and overlook the incidents we do not understand. We see our lives as sane and logical, and all else must be fiction."

"But it's not," Elizabeth whispered back. "There's something more."

"It is our cross to bear," said Dr. O'Malley, "to believe, when others do not. To use the tools of science for things that seem irrational. To record this litany of incredible events—and, when necessary, to intervene."

"Intervene?"

"As you did with Miss Greyson," said Dr. O'Malley. "Where the uncanny would do us harm, we must defy it."

"But why sixteen generations?" implored Elizabeth. "Where did it come from?"

"We've talked enough," said Dr. O'Malley. "Now we'll get some shuteye. And God willing, we'll wrest Sir Shanley from his troubles, and he'll explain the rest—just as he once explained it to me."

❖

Elizabeth woke from a deep, dreamless slumber. She staggered from her guest room and rubbed her crusted eyes. She tapped at Dr. O'Malley's door, then opened it. The room was empty, except for the remade bed and a pair of opened suitcases.

The corridor was also empty. Elizabeth scoured the house for signs of life. No one emerged. Even Lady Shanley was nowhere to be found. Elizabeth descended the staircase and passed through the empty atrium. Only when she rounded a corner into the dining room did she spot Dr. O'Malley, seated at the long table.

Dr. O'Malley was dressed in a black evening coat and necktie. His shirt was crisp white. He had probably saved these garments for a formal occasion, packing them in the undermost reaches of his luggage. He was showered, his hair oiled and combed. A napkin was tucked neatly into his collar. Even from a distance, Elizabeth sniffed a dab of cologne.

He held a knife and fork above a large round plate. A half-eaten steak floated in a pool of mushroom sauce, along with peas and an emptied potato skin. The sight of Elizabeth startled him. He choked down the sinewy meat, ripped the napkin from his neck, and struggled to stand up from the heavy chair.

"Good evening!" he exclaimed.

"No need for decorum," Elizabeth muttered, seating herself across from him. "How's the grub?"

"The *grub*," said Dr. O'Malley, rolling his tongue inside his cheek, "is delicious."

Lexi emerged from the kitchen. She stood at attention. "Good evening, miss," she said. "Do you have an appetite?"

"Do I ever," said Elizabeth. "I'll have what he's having."

A steaming dish arrived, and Elizabeth's stomach roared with hunger. The utensils shook in her hand as she quartered the meat, stuffing chunks into her mouth. Savory flavors flooded her taste buds; she relished the potato covered in cream and minced chives.

Lexi returned with a bottle of wine. "Is everything to your liking?"

"Compliments to the chef," Elizabeth replied. She masticated for a moment, then added, "And—thank you, Lexi."

Lexi answered with a faint smile. Elizabeth regretted being so tepid before. She'd been tired. Agitated. She didn't like all these secrets. What had Lexi offered but more mysteries atop mysteries? And—though she hated to think it—the girl was pretty, she supposed. She'd never known how to behave around pretty girls, cowering servant or otherwise. The way Dr. O'Malley spoke to her, so soothing and kind, made her prickle. Not jealousy, exactly, but maybe something like—

"Do you cook much?" Dr. O'Malley asked.

"Me?" Elizabeth said. "I... *burn* things."

Lexi giggled. She slapped a hand over her mouth, but the giggle persisted.

"I'm really very good at it," Elizabeth added. "Give me any ingredient you like—ham, eggs, a Thanksgiving turkey. I'll turn it into charcoal."

Lexi tried to contain her amusement. "Will there be anything else?" she asked, setting the wine bottle on the table.

"Yes," said Elizabeth. "Why don't you fetch another glass and take a seat?"

Dr. O'Malley stopped chewing. Lexi stared. The room felt suddenly still and airless.

"Oh, come now," Elizabeth chided. "Who's to know? The Shanleys aren't even here. And what difference does it make? You've served a thousand meals here. You might as well enjoy one."

Lexi flushed. "Oh, I don't... that is..."

"*Come* now," coaxed Elizabeth. "We don't bite. Unless you're a steak, that is."

Dr. O'Malley sipped his wine, bemused. He raised his glass toward an empty chair. "I suppose we're playing by American rules tonight."

Lexi didn't take this invitation lightly. She hesitated for a long minute, seeming to hold her breath. Then she sidestepped, ever so slowly, into the kitchen. Elizabeth thought she might stay there, hidden with the cook; but finally she returned, clutching a wine glass and plateful of food. She arranged them on the table and wriggled into the seat. Lexi slouched painfully. Elizabeth doubted the girl had ever sat down in any chair in the entire house.

Elizabeth pushes away her knife and fork. "All right, then. I think it's time somebody asked the question."

"The question?" returned Dr. O'Malley.

"What's the matter with Lady Shanley?"

She half-expected Dr. O'Malley to scold her for being so blunt. Yet the professor only dabbed his mouth with a napkin. He said, "Trauma, perhaps."

"Trauma? Really?"

"I suspect she knows that Teddy's out," reflected Dr. O'Malley, "but I doubt she knows where or why. Never underestimate the power of denial, especially in a house like this one."

"Did you know her—before?"

"No," answered Dr. O'Malley. "I knew *of* her. But in those days Sir Shanley had an office. He kept his professional life quite separate. I only met her once. He hosted an anniversary party for an admiral he knew. I can't imagine why *I* was invited. I never opened my mouth, for fear that they'd arrest me for trespassing."

"It doesn't make *sense*," Lexi blurted.

When both pairs of eyes turned to her, she bit her lip.

"Go on," said the professor.

"Well—a gentleman like that? He fancied the drink, of course. Every man does. But opium? That's for derelicts and dockers."

"It does seem strange," concurred Dr. O'Malley. "And it contradicts everything I've known of him. But men do change. It's been some years, and age affects each man a different way."

"His letters sounded more despondent," Elizabeth asserted. "Or that's how they read to me."

Dr. O'Malley tossed the napkin on the table, straightened his tie, and rose to his feet. "Well, I, for one, am tired of questions. It's high time we find some answers."

❖

A pair of drunkards tottered toward them. They burst into phlegmy laughter, and their breath dissipated in the moist air. One man sang a few bars, and the other tried to harmonize. Failing to remember the lyrics, they clapped each other on the chest and laughed harder. Each had an arm over the other's shoulder, and together they zigzagged down the street, stopping only long enough to spit in the murky darkness.

Elizabeth watched them approach. This was her first glimpse of Lilac Way, and the teetering drunks looked like a standard sample. One of the men swiveled sideways and tried to focus his eyes on her. His mouth agape, the man slurred, "Going our way, love?"

"I certainly hope not," countered Elizabeth.

Elizabeth knew she should fear such burly lushes, but she felt confident she could outrun them—or even knock them over, their feet were so unsteady. Yet the men only chortled, blathered something to each other, and staggered round a brick corner.

"Guttersnipes," cursed Dr. O'Malley.

Elizabeth shrugged. "I just wanted to hear the joke. Must've been a gas."

They crossed the street. Elizabeth heard the muffled *oompah-pah* of music behind closed doors, along with the racket of a hundred conversations, the clank of glasses, and the shouting of gamesmen at their darts and pool tables. A handful of men stood smoking in the dank alleyways. They passed spectral figures in scally caps, their hands deeply pocketed in woolen slacks. A strange feeling came over Elizabeth—not the dread she had expected, but a surge of excitement. She scanned the dog-eared posters on rugged walls; the ads for burlesque shows; the windows filled in with brick; the blend of mist and smoke that wafted past the streetlamps. She savored the clutter on the steps, the rubbish in the street, the lonely barrels and drums, the pipes that jutted out of crumbling masonry. She spotted a handful of men gathered on a rickety staircase, throwing dice on the wooden landing. The landscape should appall her, yet Elizabeth was mesmerized. This was the place that good girls never went. This was the world that a professor's daughter was never supposed to see.

Lexi didn't look so charmed. She pulled her scarf tighter around her face. She trotted around puddles, her eyes darting in all directions. Elizabeth wondered what the poor girl had seen, cutting her way through slums like this.

"Over there," Lexi whispered. "That's the one he frequented."

The building was the same as all the others, a shadowy hulk with a large wood door. A sign dangled over the street, its surface embossed with Chinese characters. A serpentine red dragon curled its body around the circumference of the sign; its nostrils blew rings of smoke.

A man stood outside, his hands clasped behind his back. He was young and skinny; his attempt to grow a goatee looked like pencil shavings around his mouth. He hunched inside his loose-fitting *changshan*, and his arms dangled with boredom.

"Greetings," said Dr. O'Malley, removing his cap. "We're here to collect our friend."

The youth blinked at Dr. O'Malley. "What name?" he snapped.

"Sir Shanley."

The man's eyebrows arched. "Shanley?" he said. His accent was thick, and it took Elizabeth a moment to realize he'd repeated the colonel's name. He jabbed a finger at Dr. O'Malley. "You talk Master Fung."

He threw open the door and waved them inside. Dr. O'Malley plunged into the dark corridor, followed by Lexi— and before she knew what was happening, Elizabeth followed close behind.

At the end of the black tunnel, a room emerged. Stained glass lanterns dangled from the ceiling, their bulbs glowing dimly. They cast a somber light over the collection of sofas and rugs. Across each piece of furniture reclined a separate human form. Patrons were wrapped in lavish blankets; some were naked, cloaked only in shadows. Hair blossomed from flabby chests; breasts tumbled sideways; legs were bent at Romanesque angles; afghans were slyly draped over nether regions. Opium pipes were everywhere, with handles of ebony and ivory, silver and bamboo. Their bowls were carved into elephant heads and demon faces, knots and hieroglyphs. Patrons dipped their pipes into opium lamps on the floor. They sucked the smoke into their lungs, exhaling with practiced ease, like artists painting the air with their vapor. Women in kimonos knelt on the floor, their knees pressed into pillows, as they helped fit pipes into waiting lips. Their faces were painted like dolls; their hair was wrapped and coiled. Their fingers held each apparatus with delicate care. An eerie sweetness permeated the fog—a syrupy incense that made Elizabeth feel faint. The gallery was subdued, except for the heavy respirations; the slow slither of limbs; the low moans of fleeting ecstasy. Never had the sight of decadence so amazed her.

The Chinese doorman easily cut his way through the human debris, his slippers padding noiselessly over Persian rugs. Elizabeth followed Dr. O'Malley so closely that she nearly stepped on his heels. At the far corner of the room, they passed through a beaded curtain. They filed into a tiny office—and there, seated behind a lacquered black table, sat Mr. Fung.

Whatever Elizabeth had expected, this man was not it.

Mr. Fung wore a frock coat with a velvet collar. An ascot tie was tucked into a starched white shirt. His close-cut hair was handsomely parted, and his powdery face was clean-shaven, except for an urbane mustache. He grasped a long cigarette holder in his fingers, its cherry blazing in the murk. Documents were spread out before him, each page densely printed with Chinese characters. As they entered, Mr. Fung swept these papers into a pile, clasped his hands on the table, and drew a long breath.

"Good evening," he said. "How may I help you?"

Mr. Fung did not speak in a breathy Mandarin accent; his dialect was polished, Oxfordian.

Before anyone could speak, Lexi stepped forward. She yanked down the scarf, revealing a sour grimace.

Mr. Fung leaned back in his chair, sighing heavily.

"Ah," he said, brushing ashes from his pant leg. "You've come back. And thank God—better late than never."

"Then you know why we're here?" said Dr. O'Malley.

"Of course," Mr. Fung said brusquely. "You've come for Theodore. At least I *hope* that's why you're here."

"Can you lead us to him? We'll be happy to pay his bill and be on our way."

Mr. Fung raised an eyebrow. He flicked his cigarette toward an ashtray. "His bill?"

"Yes. Whatever he owes you for the..." Dr. O'Malley struggled for the word. "For the *contraband*."

Mr. Fung pressed his fingers into a pyramid. "I see."

Dr. O'Malley flinched. "You see what?"

"I see—you really *don't* know why you're here."

Mr. Fung rose from his chair. He straightened his jacket, and his dark silhouette was reflected in the table's glassy surface. "I shall take you to him, and presently. But before we go, please understand—Theodore is my friend. And not because of *this*." He wagged a finger toward the den. "Rest assured, Sir Shanley is not one of *them*, nor has he ever been."

"He doesn't smoke opium?" asked Elizabeth.

"Absolutely *not*," bellowed Mr. Fung. "I wouldn't hear of it. I would never serve opium to a man I respect, no matter how he entreated me. I would sooner cut ties altogether than watch a friend go to ruin."

"Then where *is* he?" demanded Dr. O'Malley. "Is he not here?"

"I'll show you," said Mr. Fung. "But bear in mind—Theodore is not well. Opiates are one thing; his situation is quite another. What you are about to see will not make sense—at first. But listen to me, and once you understand, you shall see—*I'm on your side.*"

❖

Mr. Fung led them down a hallway. Cobwebs clung to corners; carpet and molding were decrepit with age. He stopped at a hefty bookcase, its shelves laden with forgotten volumes. It looked lonely, standing halfway down the naked corridor.

Mr. Fung gripped one side of the bookcase with both hands. For a moment, Elizabeth wanted to say, *What's this? A secret passage?* But then, to her amazement, the bookcase actually moved, and the sliver of an opening emerged.

"Nice cover," she murmured.

The room was a small parlor. Landscape paintings decorated the walls. Potted ferns billowed in the corners. A ceramic stand was packed with umbrellas. The walls were ringed with shelves and sideboards. Like the rest of the establishment, there were no windows at all; any light emanated from stained glass lamps.

There were also people.

In the middle of the room, five thick chairs were arranged in a circle. Their backs were slanted, like barber chairs, so their five occupants could comfortably recline. Each figure lay back, head lolling sideways, lost in fathoms of sleep.

But before Elizabeth could think to identify these strangers, she noticed the room's centerpiece—a large metal box.

The cube was nearly the size of a steamer trunk, topped with helical cables. Two antennae protruded from its center; blue ribbons of electricity crackled upward, bridging the gap between the two rods, until they sparked into nothingness. Elizabeth savored the sizzle and pop of unleashed energy.

From the center of the box, a tangle of skinny wires radiated outward. They rambled over the carpet and coiled upward. The wires rested on the clothes of the slumbering quintet, snaking all the way to their heads. And there, each wire ended in a small needle—inserted into the skin of their faces.

Needles were everywhere—lanced into temples and cheeks, into necks and throats. Needles pierced behind their earlobes; needles stuck sideways into their brows. Their eyes shifted busily behind their closed lids. Their fingers twitched. A shoulder flinched, then a foot.

There were two women—one, a raven-haired beauty in an evening gown. The other was a dark-skinned woman in a bright sari, her hair covered in a floral scarf. Next to her, a middle-aged man wore a silk *sherwani* tunic. A second man sat beside them, young and heavily bearded, with high boots and a blue hunting jacket.

And there, on the far side of the room, sat Sir Shanley.

His cheeks were sunken. His muttonchops were scraggly and overgrown. His billowed white shirt was split open, revealing a pale chest. His arms were reduced to twigs. His flesh puddled over his bones like oversized clothes. Except for the glacial rise of his chest, the man could have been mistaken for dead.

"Jumping Jehosephat!" whispered Dr. O'Malley. "Teddy—what have they done to you?"

"What *we've done*," said Mr. Fung, sternly, "is keep our friend alive."

Dr. O'Malley ripped off his spectacles. "And what does *that* mean?"

"What you see here," said Mr. Fung, "this place—is a *Somalodge*."

"Dear *God*," whispered Dr. O'Malley. "So they *do* exist."

"Exist?" Mr. Fung sneered. "They've become quite popular."

"Popular or not," interjected Elizabeth, "I haven't the faintest idea what you two are talking about."

❖

A servant arrived and set down a tea service. Lexi, Elizabeth, and Dr. O'Malley had no chairs, so they leaned against the sideboards. Mr. Fung poured steaming liquid and distributed it among the tiny cups.

"The idea is really quite simple," began Mr. Fung. "Suppose you are a child, and you're playing a game. You call it *knights and castles*. You pick up a stick and pretend it's a sword. You call yourself Sir Galahad, and you gallop about the yard on a hobby horse. Soon, your mates join in. You're all playing together, now. You pretend to fight a dragon. You pretend to save the princess. None of this is real, but your imaginations intertwine. You share your vision."

"Of course," interrupted Dr. O'Malley. "Schoolyard games. What of it?"

"But consider the *mind*," said Mr. Fung, his eyes wide with ardor. "What *is* the mind? It is energy. It is electrical currents. We Chinese have known this for millennia. Now, suppose you could combine the current from one mind with the current of another. You imagine yourselves in the same place, at the same time. Your minds share a fantasy." Mr. Fung gestured to the needles sticking out of the bearded man's face. "And you join them together with *acupuncture*."

"Yet are they not asleep?" objected Dr. O'Malley. "How do they control their dreams, any more than the rest of us do?"

"It's not exactly sleep," said Mr. Fung. "Nor it is precisely a dream. They have entered a deliberate trance. Their visions are lucid. They know where they really are and what is happening. If they walk through a fire, they will not feel its burn. If they eat a meal, its taste will fail to satisfy them. And when they wish to leave the dreamscape, they have only to concentrate, and they shall wake."

"Fine, then," blustered Dr. O'Malley. "Let's wake him up!"

Dr. O'Malley moved toward Sir Shanley, but Mr. Fung stepped between them. He grasped Dr. O'Malley's arm. "But that's the hitch, my friend—*we* can't rouse him."

"Poppycock!" blurted Dr. O'Malley.

"*Look*, O'Malley! An electrical current is running through his brain. He is deeply invested in his subconscious. If you tear him away, there is no telling what damage it could wreak."

"But why do they do it?" asked Elizabeth. "What's the point of all this?"

"The point?" Mr. Fung smiled strangely. "Entertainment, my dear. A diversion. An escape from the world. Perhaps you are too young to understand. Or perhaps life has rewarded you enough. But a Somalodge is a place of sanctuary. You leave behind the drudgery of life. You *create a world*, and you share that world with others. You can do what you like, and at the timeless pace of a dream. What could be more wondrous?"

"How long do they stay?" Elizabeth said.

"Ah, an excellent question," replied Mr. Fung. "Most stay for a day or two. Some for a couple of hours. These Brahmans arrived last night. The bearded fellow came this morning. They are all happily exploring the world they have created together. To them, weeks have passed. Months, perhaps. I expect they'll wake sometime this evening—but they shall *feel* as if they've been away quite some time."

"What about Sir Shanley?"

Mr. Fung darkened. "That, my dear, is the source of all our woes. Theodore came three weeks ago."

"Three *weeks*," Dr. O'Malley intoned. "You mean to tell me he's been slumped in that chair for twenty days, and no one has thought to bring him back?"

"Mind your tone, sir," Mr. Fung shot back. "We've *all* thought to bring him back. We have *urged* him to come back. All our recent guests have met him in the dreamscape. They beseech him to wake. But he refuses. They say he is content. In his mind, he lives quite happily. But out here, his body..." Mr. Fung sighed. "Well, you can see. He has wasted away. And he won't last much longer."

"How have you kept him alive?" asked Elizabeth.

"We use a feeding tube."

"A feeding tube," echoed Dr. O'Malley. "So it's come to that, has it?"

The only sound in the room was the zip of electricity above the mysterious box.

At last Elizabeth cleared her throat. "*I'll* go talk to him."

Dr. O'Malley slammed down his tea cup. "Elizabeth! Surely not. I ought to be the one."

"No, you *oughtn't*, actually."

"Elizabeth, you've never even met the man!"

"That might work to our advantage."

"What sense does that make?"

"It makes sense," said Elizabeth fiercely, "because *he doesn't want to live anymore.*"

Another silence fell over the room. No one made a sound.

"Isn't it obvious?" said Elizabeth. "*Look* at him. He's spent three weeks in a trance. He stopped writing you, professor. He deserted his wife. What does he care whether you feed him or not? He's made his decision. He wants to stay there until his body gives out. He's given up on everyone he knows. But maybe—just *maybe*—a stranger can do what a friend can't."

They all exchanged glances. But there was nothing to debate. Dr. O'Malley scowled. None of this was part of his plan. The whole situation had gotten out of hand.

But then he looked up. He gazed on his mentor with pained eyes. Slowly, he nodded his assent. The others nodded back, a silent, unanimous vote. Absurd as their situation was, they all knew what must now be done.

❖

"To enter the dreamscape," Mr. Fung began, "there are three steps. The first is acupuncture."

Mr. Fung raised a needle into Elizabeth's field of vision. It was twice as long as a sewing needle, but only as thick as a strand of hair. Elizabeth cringed as the needle hovered over her eyes, then veered upward, into her forehead.

Elizabeth felt its prick. The point slid into her *depressor supercilii*—the triangular muscle just above her eyebrow. The pain was minuscule; she dismissed it with a blink. But as Mr. Fung applied more needles, the sensation grew strange; with each breath, she felt them jutting from her face. Each needle was weighed down by the slim cords that connected her to the electrical box.

At last Mr. Fung stepped back and examined his work.

"How do you feel?" he asked.

"Like a pincushion."

Mr. Fung smiled at this. His servant appeared again—a humorless girl in a geisha's dress. She presented Mr. Fung with a weathered wood box. Mr. Fung set down the box, lifted the lid, and revealed a long black pipe. The apparatus was a plain little thing, resting in a bed of crushed velvet.

"The second step," Mr. Fung continued, "is *cannabis sativa.*"

"*Cannabis!*" Dr. O'Malley bellowed. "You can't be serious."

"Cannabis eases the mind," Mr. Fung replied coolly. "It will help her enter the dreamscape."

"You said no opiates!" retorted Dr. O'Malley.

"Calm yourself, my friend. You have nothing to fear. Cannabis is not an opiate, despite what they say. She needs only a puff, and her subconscious will do the rest."

Elizabeth watched the long-stemmed pipe emerge from the box. She had never seen cannabis before, and she had little idea what it looked like. Mr. Fung pinched a green splotch between his fingers; it looked like a tiny green tumbleweed, the withered leaves wrapped into a tight ball. Mr. Fung stuffed the cannabis into the chamber, then looked up at Elizabeth.

"You have nothing to fear, my dear," Mr. Fung said, with disarming gentleness. "Nothing you are about to experience can harm you, any more than a dream."

He angled the pipe toward her. A match flared. The flame quivered, a mesmerizing dance. "Are you ready?"

"Ready as I'll ever be," said Elizabeth.

"Just inhale, my dear. Deep as you can."

Never in her life had Elizabeth anticipated a moment like this—reclined in a chair, in a secret anteroom, in an opium den, in a small town in England. Elizabeth, of all people—the sullen outcast, the jaded genius in the back of the room—was the last person anyone would have imagined in this situation.

What would her schoolmates have thought, back in Pittsburgh? Would they ever believe her story, about the Chinese druggist who offered her a forbidden pipe? In an instant, Elizabeth recalled all the horror stories she'd ever heard—reefer addicts losing their minds in tenement houses, smashing their belongings, beating their neighbors, hurling themselves out of windows. How would she handle the throes of marijuana? Would O'Malley have to restrain her? Once lost, would she ever regain her senses? Would she forever be known as the girl who ruined her mind, a cautionary tale for defiant youths?

The hell with it, she thought.

Elizabeth bit down on the pipe's stem. She inhaled, and a deluge of smoke poured into her mouth, down her throat, filling her lungs. Then she exhaled, and she felt the jet of smoke seep out. It felt easy, good.

A new sensation flooded her consciousness—her brain seemed to expand inside her skull, fizzing, lifting, defying gravity. She felt airy and light, as if her soul was steaming through her pores, a mist of being and non-being; gravity and weightlessness; cognizance and oblivion. Her eyes were speckled with color, amorphous shapes, dots and specters. They curved into a tunnel, and she felt herself gliding into it, dimensionless, ethereal, a fractal among fractals.

Mr. Fung's distant voice spoke: "The final step is the zoetrope…"

His voice echoed through her cerebellum—*zoetrope, zoetrope, ZOETROPE, ZOETROPE…*

Somehow, through the hallucinatory fog, Elizabeth could see the apparatus set down before her. It was a cylinder, perhaps two feet wide and one foot tall, with slits cut into its curved side. Elizabeth had seen a zoetrope before, years earlier, at the carnival. She remembered the man with the twirled mustache and monocle, his beaming grin and striped shirt. *Would you like to see the horsey run?* he'd asked. Then he'd spun the zoetrope around. Through the slats, she could see the sequential photographs of a horse. Each picture blended with the others. The horse seemed to run in place, its hooves pounding the soil, picking up speed from a trot to a gallop. She remembered this all so clearly now—

"Just look," said Mr. Fung. His voice echoed—*just look, just look, just loooooook.*

Mr. Fung spun the zoetrope. There was no horse. Instead, it was a dusty road. People wandered across the dry pavement. There were palm trees swaying in the hot breeze. A golden spire rose into the sky. It was a palace, with tiered and sloping rooftops. Elizabeth studied the building— imperious, exotic—shaped like a tall pagoda. Serpentine dragons wreathed its doorway. She could feel a warm tide in her forehead, like the flow of water through her mind. She felt herself smile.

And then—*she was there.*

She heard the squawk of birds; the march of sandaled feet; the roll of oxcarts; the bray of a donkey. The sounds were muffled, but unmistakable. She saw passersby, blurred at first, but easing into focus. Men in conical hats scuttled across the street; they held long poles, pulled wheelbarrows, heaved bags onto their shoulders. Elizabeth meandered through the crowd, until she found the steps of the palace.

Its central spire towered above her, dark against the red-and-violet clouds. Elizabeth climbed the steps, pausing only long enough to notice the palace guards. They stood at attention, heavily armored and holding halberds at their sides. They didn't move. They said nothing. Whatever this palace was, Elizabeth was welcome to enter.

All at once, Elizabeth swelled with confidence. *This is all an illusion*, she thought. *This is all a dream.* She crouched low and touched the stone step. Her fingertips sensed the step, but she didn't *feel* its texture, its hardness, its sunbaked heat. This numbness reassured her. This place posed no danger. Nothing could harm her. She was mistress of the realm, as entitled as any other dreamer.

Elizabeth continued her ascent. Slowly, she felt something else—a magnetic pull, a rush of familiarity. But how could this be? She had never been here. She had spent only a few minutes in the dream. Or *was* it a few minutes? How much time had actually elapsed? She could barely remember the stairway that had already passed beneath her feet. When she arrived at the tall gateway, the red doors groaned open; by the time she had resolved to step forward, she had already moved through the door and was standing inside the palace. Here, time and space were different. The minutes were vague approximations. Her movement was lazy and imprecise.

Elizabeth made her way down the corridor, drawn by a gravity she didn't understand. Then she remembered—this world was a *collaboration*. She couldn't see the others, but she could sense them. She could feel their minds tethered together, the melding of their collective knowledge. The palace walls looked so familiar, as if she'd drawn them on a sheet of paper. Elizabeth remembered so many expressions just then—*déjà vu, the feeling you've done something before; presque vu, the feeling of an impending epiphany; déjà entendu, the feeling you have heard a sound*—

Elizabeth halted. She saw movement down the wide stone hallway.

A figure sauntered toward her. The profile was tall, muscled, masculine. A red house robe billowed around his frame. Yet as the figure approached, Elizabeth doubted her own eyes. His face was large and black. Two lumps appeared on each side—ears. Soft green eyes smoldered in the dim light. Whiskers sprouted from a leonine nose.

The head was a black panther.

The shape of his body was human, but even his skin was covered in rich fur. Brawny arms swung at his side; his hands were feline paws. Baggy *sirwal* trousers covered his legs, and a long tail wagged behind him. His movement was a perfect synthesis of man and animal. It took all of Elizabeth's courage to hold her ground.

The panther stopped. He stood only a few paces in front of Elizabeth. They faced each other silently. Half the panther's face was lit scarlet from the setting sun; the other half was lost in shadow.

"Good evening, my dear," he said. His voice was low and placid, like the lap of the ocean on a rocky shore. "Are you new here?"

"I've come to find Sir Shanley," said Elizabeth. As she spoke, she decided she disliked the sound of her own voice—tinny and distant, as if recorded on a wax cylinder.

The panther cocked his head to the side, studying her. His eyes expressed curiosity, nothing more.

"Is Teddy expecting you?"

"Does it matter?"

The creature seemed to consider this. At last, he shrugged and turned around. Elizabeth followed him down the hall. The setting sun blinded her, but its synthetic warmth and glare didn't irk her the way the real sun would. Just when she felt mesmerized by the rhythm of their muted footsteps, a table and chairs came into view.

There he was. Sir Shanley, seated in a wicker chair.

The man leaned forward, and Elizabeth was startled to behold his healthy figure. Sir Shanley looked fleshy, sanguine, fit as a fiddle. His cheeks were plump, his hair a sandy gray. Seeing Sir Shanley hunched over his marble table and its many board games, Elizabeth imagined him as her own relative, some great-uncle.

Sir Shanley looked up. He smiled simply, then hiked up the sleeves of his robe. He grasped a bottle of champagne, pouring its contents into a flute.

"Well, hello," he said in a husky baritone. "Welcome to my palace."

❖

Dr. O'Malley squeezed a penny in his fist. It was something he always did, when he wanted a drink and couldn't have one. He had left his holster in a drawer, back in the guestroom's bureau, but knowing its whereabouts hardly cured his temptation. Dr. O'Malley assumed that Mr. Fung's cabinet was well stocked; but liquor was the last thing he needed—one tipple always demanded another. Normally, he could subsist on tea, the same bland stuff he was sipping now. Normally, he could go for days without a craving. Yet on the road, under such duress, Dr. O'Malley's thirst for scotch was relentless. Pressing his fingertips into a copper coin was the only ritual that had ever worked. *Sobriety only costs me a penny*, he used to joke. *But God save me if I ever run out of change.*

The room was warm and stuffy, and Mr. Fung and Dr. O'Malley were sweating. Lexi's face was dry, even though she still wore her scarf, and the professor wondered about her circulation. Behind her, a handsome clock stood on a sideboard. Dr. O'Malley had barely noticed it before, but now its face maddened him; the clock's second hand crawled from minute to minute. Time moved so slowly that Dr. O'Malley thought the clock might be broken.

"*Entertainment*," Dr. O'Malley scoffed. "Such a tragic way to go."

Mr. Fung was polishing his ring with a rag. He frowned at Dr. O'Malley. "I shan't disagree. I myself feel a bit hoodwinked."

"Hoodwinked? How so?"

"I've known Theodore for some years now," said Mr. Fung, slipping the ring back onto his finger. "Not as long as you, I imagine. But when my family came to Nestershire, he was kind to my father. His kindness meant the world to us, and we never forgot his favors. We were exiles, and the English reviled my family. It was a desperate time for us, and only Sir Shanley lent his hand. It was his encouragement—and his formal recommendation—that paved my way to Cambridge. To put it mildly, I owe the man a great deal."

"Might I ask what you studied?" said Dr. O'Malley irritably. "That you should open an opium den?"

Mr. Fung absorbed the backhanded insult with a grin. "This establishment was my father's. I was raised under this very roof, as shameful as it sounds. I used to watch my father make deposits in the safe. He would keep it behind a painting in his office." Mr. Fung paused, lost in the memory. "To answer your question, I studied engineering. I have always loved the mechanics of things. But let me ask you, Dr. O'Malley, for you seem an educated man—what English university would welcome *you*, an Irishman, with open arms? What dean would entrust you with teaching the sons of England? Would they even allow you through the gates? Or would they just as soon frisk you for weapons?" When Dr.

O'Malley looked away, Mr. Fung said, "We're in the same boat, my friend. Years ago, I was foolish enough to believe than a London firm might hire me. I could almost picture it. I'd be out there building bridges, amongst my English peers. But all they ever saw in me was the Yellow Peril. They laughed at my name. They threw soiled clothes at me. They spread their eyes and spoke in gibberish. Their mockery exhausted me. So I came back here. I took over my father's work. Now I give the *laowei* what he wants—a little wad of dried poppies, and a pipe to smoke it from.

"But the Somalodge," Mr. Fung went on, his tone lightening, "is something else entirely. I designed it myself, with some help from friends in Manchester. Say what you will, but there is nothing purer than the mind. And to share your mind with others? What could be more beautiful? What gift, more intimate?"

For an instant, Dr. O'Malley stole a glimpse at Lexi. The desire—to look at her—had nagged him since their arrival; only now did he succumb.

Then, to his puerile delight, Lexi glanced back. Their eyes met for only an instant, and then they bounced away. Lexi pushed a curl of hair behind her ear; she pulled her knit cap tighter. But Dr. O'Malley's pulse throbbed in his temples. He hated to admit it, but everything Mr. Fung said made sense. If only circumstances were different, how much would he love to merge his daydreams with hers?

"To his credit," Mr. Fung said quietly, "I don't know how Theodore learned of the Somalodge. Perhaps a friend told him. At any rate, *he* came to *me*. I was surprised. I welcomed him, of course, and I honored his request. To me, that was all it was. I know he has a fondness for curios. He likes…" Mr. Fung searched the ceiling for the right word. "He likes *esoteric* things. So I obliged."

"But he came back."

"He did. Many times. For a few hours, at first, then a full evening. Each time, he looked so happy, so alive. I should say, he looked *younger*. But I cautioned him. I advised some respite, between each session. I even lied to him sometimes, insisting the room was full, just to defer his visits. I urged moderation. I thought he understood. But then…"

"He stayed."

"Yes. I should have known better."

Dr. O'Malley gritted his teeth. He couldn't help himself. He sneered, "Perhaps you should have."

Suddenly, Dr. O'Malley heard a feminine gasp. His head jerked sideways, toward the bodies slumped in their chairs.

One of the figures sat upright, eyes wide, mouth agape. She sucked in air, and her hands drifted upward, toward her forehead. Instinctively, she began to touch the needles protruding from her face. Mr. Fung threw himself across the room. He touched her shoulders, then guided her wrists back into her lap.

"Please, Miss Maybell," he said soothingly. "Allow me."

It was the raven-haired woman, who now batted her eyes in confusion. Mr. Fung slipped a pair of gloves over his hands—thick and rubbery, the kind used for scrubbing floors. Miss Maybell winced as the needles were removed from her skin and collected into a bundle of cords. She glanced about the room, squinting at Dr. O'Malley and Lexi, but said nothing. Then she pressed a hand against her stomach, leaned toward Mr. Fung, and whispered something into his ear.

"Of course," Mr. Fung said.

The woman stood up, but her legs wobbled beneath her. She stepped awkwardly around the other guests and pushed through the secret doorway, into the corridor.

"Where is she going?" asked Dr. O'Malley.

"The water closet," answered Mr. Fung. "She's been sitting here for quite some time. More than a day, in fact."

Dr. O'Malley screwed up his face. For all their scientific talk, he hadn't considered a full bladder. This consequence of the Somalodge had not occurred to him. Not only had Mr. Fung been forced to feed Sir Shanley, but he must have tended to all of the man's bodily functions. Now the professor felt a pang of sympathy for Mr. Fung, who could just as easily have wrested Sir Shanley from his dreams and thrown him in the street. It took commitment to keep such a comatose man alive. Dr. O'Malley regretted his stormy attitude, his accusations. He could never condone the opium, but was the Somalodge so vile? Could Dr. O'Malley begrudge Sir Shanley—his yearning to escape, to exist in another world, to refashion his existence in a more perfect way?

Dr. O'Malley drew his tobacco pipe and lit it.

A few minutes later, the lady re-entered. She still looked shaken. Her eyes darted about the room, and she rubbed her arm nervously. Dr. O'Malley felt the urge to calm her. He nodded and said, "Good evening, miss."

"Good evening," the woman replied. Her face was colorless; her hair was clumped with sweat. "Will you be taking my place?"

"Oh, no," Dr. O'Malley said. "I'm here—that is, *we're* here—to meet with Sir Shanley."

"Sir Shanley," the lady echoed distantly. "You mean Theodore?"

"Precisely! Have you seen him?"

"I—I just left him."

"How is he?" Dr. O'Malley burst. "Is he all right?"

The lady hesitated a moment before stepping forward, toward her empty chair. She removed her fur coat from the chair's back and wriggled into it, then collected her handbag. She studied the room. Her eyes drifting to Mr. Fung, to the bodies still seated, to the two strange spectators. She was dazed, confused. She wavered slightly, her eyelids drooping, and for a moment Dr. O'Malley thought she might collapse.

"Mr. Fung," Miss Maybell intoned. "This was a *wondrous* experience. There is no other word for it. I feel I've been away for years. A *lifetime*. I am beholden to you, Mr. Fung, for introducing me to this… phenomenon."

"You are always welcome, Miss Maybell."

"But I fear I shan't be back," Miss Maybell added quickly. "A little perfection is a dangerous thing."

"*Please*," implored Dr. O'Malley, stepping toward her with open palms. "Before you go, tell me—is Teddy all right? Did he say anything?"

"He did," choked Miss Maybell. A gust of emotion blew through her. "And believe me—he's *never* coming back. I can tell. He'd sooner die."

With this, she turned m toward the door. She slumped out of the room, leaving a silent void.

In such stagnant air, Dr. O'Malley was reluctant to even swallow. Her words sank in, and he knew the others thinking the same thing—*he'd sooner die*.

In a flash, Dr. O'Malley remembered all those years together—hunkered over books, filing documents, receiving telegrams from all over the world. Sir Shanley's office had been an attic, rented out of a vacant Victorian house. Multiple padlocks had barred the only entrance, and many of the documents were transcribed in code or invisible ink. Together, they had sorted through the jumble of mail, absorbing so much of the world's knowledge. Every envelope contained some astonishing secret, a truth that would shock any man on the street. He would venture home each evening, back to his cramped flat, giddy with the things he had learned.

He owed his life to Sir Shanley. And so did Lexi, and Mr. Fung, and so many others. Yet now, here he was—wilting in a recumbent chair. Allowing himself to die. That pasty carcass looked nothing like the plucky man he had known. How had his mentor fallen so far? How could he squander such a full and noble life? How could he entomb himself in this glum chamber and wither to nothing?

Lexi harrumphed. "Well, there's only one thing left to do," she said.

"What do you mean?" said Dr. O'Malley.

"We've got to pull him out. By *force*."

❖

"Would you care for a seat?" offered Sir Shanley.

In a flash, Elizabeth realized the gravity of her response. There were many ways she could accept this invitation; a great deal depended on the impression she made in these first few minutes. She thought to appear docile, to coax him with kindness and flattery. But that felt unnatural; she'd never sustain the role. Or she could just be herself—an unimpressed schoolgirl—and prod him into conversation. But *that* didn't feel right, either. A man like Sir Shanley would respect neither pushover nor brat.

She must choose a new persona. Someone in the middle. Herself, but even more so.

Elizabeth plopped into a chair. She threw one leg over the other. She said, "Sir Shanley, I presume?"

"I am," he said. "And you are?"

"Elizabeth." She examined her nails in the pale sunlight. "They tell me you were a general."

All movement ceased. Sir Shanley was about to sip from his champagne, but the glass never reached his lips.

"Colonel."

"Ah," said Elizabeth. "Same as my grandfather."

"Oh? Which regiment?"

"The Seventh Calvary. He fought in the Indian Wars."

"The…" Sir Shanley leaned forward. "The *American* Indian Wars, you mean?"

"All the same to me," said Elizabeth. "Where were *you?*"

"I?" Sir Shanley smirked reflectively. "Here and about. But Burma, mostly."

Elizabeth glanced around the great hall. "I take it you liked it there."

Sir Shanley leaned back into his cushioned chair. "I suppose I did."

Elizabeth glanced beyond Sir Shanley, where a boy, perhaps ten years old, stood at attention. He wore a loose-fitting saffron outfit, and his baby-face was neutral.

"Because *he*"—Elizabeth tossed a finger at the boy— "must be someone real."

"Maung? Yes, he's my houseboy. Or *was*, at any rate."

"But this fellow here…" Elizabeth clapped a hand on the panther's shoulder; she could feel his muscles tense. "*He's* a different story, isn't he? Maybe a little more—metaphorical?"

"Larimer," Sir Shanley murmured. For an instant, he looked confused. Questioning. But he shook the feeling off. He turned stern eyes back to her. "Elizabeth, was it?"

"Crowne, yes."

"Aren't you a bit young to be dallying about a place like this?"

Elizabeth pinched a wad of hair. "Well, isn't that the point of a *place like this?* We can be whatever we like, yes? Couldn't I make myself a ravishing thirty-year-old, if I felt so inclined?"

"But you don't," snapped Sir Shanley. Then, more gently: "You *don't* choose to be older than you are, I mean."

"I like my age." Elizabeth said, unconvincingly. "To be honest, I'm not much different here than I am—well, *out there*."

"Well," said Sir Shanley, "you have a lifetime to cultivate your regrets."

Elizabeth narrowed her eyes at Sir Shanley. "Is that what Larimer is?"

Sir Shanley fell silent. Elizabeth had struck a nerve. But now she must tread carefully. Any more aggression might shut him up for good. The man was slippery; he had cultivated more than regret all these years. Even as he reposed, Sir Shanley emanated calm intelligence; she couldn't hope to combat him head-on. He could always dismiss her as a foolish child, the way all her elders wielded that obnoxious power. Elizabeth needed to catch him off-guard, to trick him into equal footing.

"Chess," said Elizabeth. She took a piece from the table and inspected it like a rare gem. "I'd love to play you, but…"

"But you're a novice," Sir Shanley concluded.

"*But*," corrected Elizabeth, "I would hate to see such a distinguished man *lose*."

A long moment elapsed. Sir Shanley looked stunned. Then he sat up straight, rubbed one eye, and said, "White or black?"

"Let's leave it to fate," Elizabeth replied. She grabbed a second piece from the table and drew her hands together. The tiny objects clattered between her palms. At last, she extended both hands, each piece hidden inside a clenched fist.

"Pick one."

"Right," said Sir Shanley.

Elizabeth retained her pose. "Right," she echoed. "But before we begin, we play by *my* rules. For every piece I capture, I ask you a question. You will answer fully and candidly—and vice versa. Agreed?"

"*That* is how I know you for an amateur," said Sir Shanley. "The point of the game is not to muck about, but to *win*."

"I like toying with opponents," said Elizabeth. "It keeps things interesting. Are we agreed?"

Sir Shanley saluted with two limp fingers. "Very well, then."

Elizabeth opened one hand and slapped a white rook against the board. "Set up your pieces. You move first."

❖

"I won't do it," declared Mr. Fung, folding his arms. "It's preposterous."

"But we must!" cried Dr. O'Malley. "He won't survive otherwise!"

"Like it not, O'Malley, the choice is *his*. We have no right. And the damage we could wreak..."

Lexi stormed forward, jutting her face into Mr. Fung's. "We *have* to try it. We *have* to. It's his only chance."

"What about the girl?" Mr. Fung said. "If she hasn't resurfaced, she must still be trying to coax him out."

"See here," Lexi rejoined. "If you don't care for the responsibility, I can respect that. He's your friend. You oughtn't do it yourself. But by God, you must tell *me* how to do it. And if it's as simple as picking them pins out of his head, I'll do it now. You needn't even watch, if you haven't the stomach for it."

Mr. Fung sighed. He stood there a long moment, his lips twisted in thought. He drew his cigarette case from his jacket pocket, but when he tried to snap it open, he fumbled, and the case fell to the floor. He gazed at them, absently. He closed his eyes.

"You'll need my gloves," he said.

❖

Elizabeth slid her bishop across the board and knocked the knight off its square. She set the captured knight on the table and said, "All right, what were you doing in Burma?"

Sir Shanley hummed through his latticed fingers. He eyes look sleepy, but Elizabeth could tell the man was preoccupied. He had advanced aggressively, invading the middle of the board, but he had only captured two pawns and a knight. Elizabeth had taken a bishop, both knights, and a rook, along with four pawns. All their remaining pieces were arranged in defensive diamonds, foreshadowing a slow and bitter battle.

"I was a civil servant," Sir Shanley said, his hand hovering indecisively over the board. "I signed documents for a living. Looked after the natives. Nothing remarkable."

"Nothing *uncanny?*"

Sir Shanley paused. He leaned back, surveying his challenger. Then, with a flick of his wrist, he took Elizabeth's pawn with his own.

"Why are *you* here?" he inquired coldly.

"Is that your question?"

"That is *indeed* my question."

Until now, their exchange had been innocent enough. Where did he come from? *London*. What had she studied in school? *Medicine*. The dialogue would have bored Elizabeth, were the stakes not so high. She had to probe Sir Shanley first, finesse him into revealing himself. His mood was delicate, as was her strategy. But could she confess her mission? Would he appreciate her honesty, or turn away for good?

"I think you know why I'm here," she said.

"If I recall your rules," Sir Shanley said, "we are to answer *fully and candidly*. I detect a breach of contract."

Larimer chuckled at this—a rich baritone of a laugh, which sounded neither human nor feline. This struck Elizabeth as strange. If Larimer was a figment, how was his behavior expressed? Did Sir Shanley operate Larimer like a marionette, deciding what the creature would do and say at any given moment? Or was Larimer autonomous, reflecting both of their imaginations at once? When he sniffed or scratched his ear, were these habits shared by the marriage of their minds?

"I wanted to meet you," said Elizabeth. She nudged a pawn forward.

"Impossible," retorted Sir Shanley. "You don't even know who I am."

"I've seen your house," retorted Elizabeth. "I've *met your wife*."

"My wife?" he sneered. "My wife is a ghost. She is an empty shell. She has only the wherewithal to feed and bathe herself, nothing more."

Elizabeth squirmed in her seat. "What do you mean?"

"What do I *mean?* I mean her mind has corroded. Senility has left her with nothing. All she knows are sensations. She follows the habits of her former life, but not for any conscious reason. The woman I married—the woman I *loved*—is gone. So no, you have *not* met my wife. You have only met the ruins that remain."

How could I have been so blind? Elizabeth thought. *No wonder she was so quiet.* That's why she never noticed his long absences. Lady Shanley was *demented*—and it was so severe that nothing he did ever mattered. Even if his actions made sense to her, the intervening minutes would wipe them from her mind. Why didn't she see it before?

"O'Malley brought you here?" Sir Shanley murmured.

Elizabeth felt her cheeks flush. "Yes."

"When you go back—as you inevitably shall—tell Professor O'Malley he has nothing to fear. I am quite content, and there is nothing he needs from me."

"He seems to disagree."

"I had hoped he would tarry longer," Sir Shanley said remorsefully. "In America, I mean. He should never have seen me like this."

Elizabeth was losing. After all this waiting, traveling, prodding, grasping at straws, she could not finagle a victory. Sir Shanley would fade into oblivion. Elizabeth would awake from this dream to find his corpse. She would fail Dr. O'Malley—and Lexi, Mr. Fung, Lady Shanley—but most especially, she would fail herself. She would have to return to that godforsaken medical school, resign herself to the insipid career Dr. O'Malley had portended. She would have to explain her fruitless month abroad, her dalliance with a mad professor, her wasted time and effort, this blundering non sequitur. Or *worse*, she would return home to Pittsburgh, known to everyone as the silly girl who had squandered her potential. She would sit in her parents' parlor, waiting for a man lonely enough to propose, and then a lackluster wedding, a humdrum house, a slew of screaming children—

"*Who is Larimer?*" she rumbled.

Sir Shanley winced. "I beg your pardon?"

"Who *is* he? And don't deny me that. You're dead, anyway, so what does it matter?"

"But…" Sir Shanley shook his head in confusion. "You have to capture a piece."

"*Stuff it*, Shanley," Elizabeth bellowed. "I'm tired of games. If you want to die, then *die*, already. I don't care anymore. But tell me who Larimer is."

"I… I think you ought to go."

"Maybe I *ought* to," Elizabeth snarled. "And anyway, you've already lost. Rook to queen four—check. Which means you have to move your king behind your bishop. Then, knight to queen five. Check mate. I could have won ten different ways by now. So by all means, waste away in your chair. Let the world forget you ever existed. Force your maid to coddle your invalid wife. Do whatever you damn well please. But tell me—*who is Larimer?*"

❖

Lexi slipped the scarf and hat from her neck, then shimmied out of her coat. She stacked the garments on a shelf, then rolled up her sleeves. She was no longer wearing the maid's outfit, but a simple wool dress. She shoved one hand into a rubber glove, struggling against its floppy shape. When Lexi had fully fitted her fingers into each black udder, she leaned forward, toward the crumpled body of Sir Shanley, and whispered to herself.

"What was that?" Mr. Fung asked. "What did you say?"

For the first time, Mr. Fung did not sound like a bastion of confidence. He smoked one cigarette after another, pouring smoke into the small room.

"I'm saying a bleeding *prayer*," Lexi snapped.

"Take your time, Lexi," Dr. O'Malley said. "We could all use a spot of divine intervention."

Lexi took a breath, squared her shoulders, and reached a hand forward. Her wrist arced in the air, and her fingers dangled ahead of her knuckles with surprising elegance. Her digits paused a few inches from Sir Shanley's face, waffling between one needle and another.

With their faces so close together, Dr. O'Malley couldn't help but notice the contrast of their features: Lexi's skin was so soft and smooth, her cheeks rosy. Her free-flowing hair looked thick and alive. Next to her, Sir Shanley looked all the more diminished—his face tautly stretched, his skin waxy and pruned. Except for his wispy breaths, Sir Shanley could have passed for a stone bust of himself.

Lexi pinched one of the needles. Her grasp was delicate, but it still sent shivers down the attached cord. Her chest sank. A sigh of relief—she had probably expected a shock, despite their preparations. The maid pulled, and the needle slid out of spotted skin. Lexi released it, and the needle fell to the floor, its cord coiling into a spring.

"One down," intoned Dr. O'Malley. "Good work, Lexi."

Lexi grasped another needle. "By the by—" she said, her voice shaking. "Where do you come from, Professor? Originally, I mean?"

"Me?" Dr. O'Malley blanched. "I… that is… Dublin, miss."

"Fancy that. My grandfather came from Galway. Small world, innit?"

Lexi looked sideways. She smiled. She smiled at *him*. Her first smile since they'd met. But it was more than that—her smile was a thin line of reassurance; sweetness; dry wit; two inches of supple lips emoted to perfection. Her eyes seemed to belong to someone entirely new—a woman who had never bowed to anyone; never scrubbed a floor on her hands and knees; never stood stoically in the corner with a tea tray. She could not have sustained the gesture for more than three seconds, but they were three seconds of dizzying euphoria— and by the time she turned her head back to the second needle, Dr. O'Malley was lost in joy.

She withdrew the needle.

Sir Shanley sputtered.

His head fell back. His back arched beneath him. Phlegm burst from his throat and blotted his collar. Every conscious person in the Somalodge jolted with surprise.

Sir Shanley's body vibrated in place. His arms jiggled at his sides. His head lolled back and forth. A yellowish froth bubbled from his mouth.

"DAMN IT!" cried Dr. O'Malley. He clambered across the room. As he moved, the professor snatched a cane from the umbrella stand. He snapped the wooden shaft over his knee, breaking it into two pieces. Then he grabbed Sir Shanley's head, narrowly avoiding the electrified needles. He squeezed the man's cheeks until his jaw came open. Then he placed the shaft horizontally across Sir Shanley's teeth.

"What's happening?" Lexi squealed.

"He's having a seizure!"

With practiced swiftness, Dr. O'Malley threw an arm over Sir Shanley's chest, bracing their shoulders against each other. The old man juddered in his chair; his knees swayed back and forth; his teeth ground into wood; saliva oozed down his cheeks. His eyelids split open; Dr. O'Malley could see his brown irises rolling underneath.

"Keep going!" commanded Dr. O'Malley.

"What?" Lexi cried, holding up her gloved hands.

"The needles! Get them out! *Now!*"

❖

Sir Shanley looked at Elizabeth. His lips were parted, his eyes unblinking. When he swallowed, Elizabeth could hear the grind of his throat. He leaned forward, as slow as a drawbridge, and set down the glass of champagne. As he rose to his feet, Sir Shanley seemed to levitate from his chair. He took a few steps and looked around. He spread his hands over his face. When he spoke, his voice came through a crosshatch of fingers.

"I was walking in the garden," Sir Shanley began. "Many years ago. A morning constitutional. That was my ritual, in Burma. Rise early, walk around a bit. It was cool, after the long rain. The sun was low in the branches. All of our trees were teak. They were so lovely, especially in the morning mist. I remember it so clearly. Quiet out, except for the birds."

He paused. His hands peeled away from his face; dropped to his sides.

"I heard a noise. It sounded like mewling. I peered through the underbrush. And there I saw him—a little black cat. At first I thought he was a stray. Perhaps he belonged to one of the coolies who lived nearby. But I looked closer, and I saw his fur coat, the shape of his head. And I knew that he was wild."

"A panther," Elizabeth whispered.

"Yes. A newborn panther. His eyes were still shut tight. He was so innocent. It was as if he had been placed there, in the shrubbery, for me to find. I didn't hesitate—I stole him from that bush and carried him to the parlor. I found a bottle of milk in the icebox. It already had a nipple affixed. I nursed him. He drank so deep, so long. He was so tiny. Such a beautiful creature. I knew he couldn't survive, alone in the jungle. So I kept him."

"For how long?"

Sir Shanley guffawed at this—a humorless sound. "How long, indeed? How long *could* I have kept him? I put him in the shed, at first. I couldn't tell my wife She would never understand. When he started to prowl about, knocking over cans, making a ruckus, I moved him to the root cellar. Every minute I could spare, I spent with him. But he grew, and kept growing. I brought him scraps, but they were never enough. After a few weeks, instincts took hold. He hid himself among the barrels. I coaxed him out, from time to time. I lured him with water and strips of meat. But he would never eat out of my hand. He would snatch the food in his teeth and run away. I wanted to pet him, to *hold* him. I wanted so many things, which I knew in my heart were impossible. I waited so long, sometimes. I called his name for hours. But it was all for nothing. He learned to conceal himself. I moved the barrels, one by one. I could hear his purr. I could sense his movement.

But I couldn't *find* him. Searching for Larimer was like a chasing a shadow. I was always too slow, too lumbering. Everywhere I looked, I imagined he had just been. It's maddening—to love something that refuses to show itself.

"So one day, I left the door open. I walked away. I cannot recall how I survived the grief. I spoke to no one. Vicky thought I was sick. She gave me chamomile tea, hoping it would revive my spirits. She is stronger than I am, you see. She can see the forest for the trees. She doesn't waste time on sentiment. But I am different. I never went to the root cellar again. Not once."

Elizabeth waited a moment. "You know what I have to ask," she said. "And you know I don't want to ask it. But I have to know—why was there a bottle of milk in your icebox? Why did it already have a nipple?"

"Because," said Sir Shanley, choking on his words, "it was supposed to be for our son."

"A newborn," said Elizabeth.

Sir Shanley nodded. He squeezed his eyes shut. "I never believed in reincarnation. When the Burmese spoke of it, I thought, 'How quaint. What *charming* people. What comforting folktales. But a man of science would never stoop to such animism.' You never believe a thing until you have to, and then you believe it with every fiber of your being. Our infant son—Larimer—was the pinnacle of my life. And then, suddenly, he was gone. He didn't survived his first week of life. I can't even remember his burial, it happened so quickly. We were too shocked to even mourn. We woke each morning, followed our routines, as if Larimer had been a dream. It might have stayed that way. We might have suppressed his loss until our final days.

"But then I saw that black kitten, lying there in the bush—and I knew that *it was him*. I had a second chance. I could make amends. I could raise that panther like a boy, because to me he *was* my boy." Sir Shanley sniffed. Tears traced the lines of his face. "I couldn't bear the thought—that he had only appeared to say goodbye."

"And then you found *this* place," Elizabeth said quietly. She looked at Larimer, whose fleecy face had turned neutral. His eyes looked blurry and his fur smudged; he was as expressionless as a doll. "You created him. All these years later. Your grown son."

"I know—" Sir Shanley croaked. "I know what this is. An illusion. A fantasy. I *know* that. But once you have experienced a dream so real—once you take stock of how little there is to return to—what choice do you have?"

"Sir Shanley," Elizabeth said, standing up to her full height. "*Teddy*. I know I'm nothing to you. I know I'm just some know-nothing girl. But Professor O'Malley needs you, which means *I* need you. This society—whatever it is—is the only thing I've ever truly wanted. I want to learn. I want to understand. Can't you see? You can always come back here. Larimer will always wait for you. There's no shame in that. But if you die now, *I'll never have what I want.* Never."

Just then, her vision shifted. The details of the room looked blotted, misshapen. Elizabeth shook her head; everything looked miscomored, redrawn in pastels. A dull ache thrummed in her brain. She doubled over, pressing hands against her temples.

"What... what was that?"

Elizabeth looked up. Sir Shanley was crouched low. One arm was wrapped around the back of his head; his fingers dug into his cheeks.

"*Damn it all,*" Sir Shanley cursed. "They're trying to pull me out."

"They're *what?*"

Sir Shanley shook his head. He crawled toward Elizabeth on hands and knees. He leaned against the edge of the table. Elizabeth lurched forward—but then her vision fizzed again. The room distorted. The ache in her forehead surged. She heard Sir Shanley wail in pain. He fell over the chessboard, knocking over the pieces. He panted into the carved grid.

"Sir Shanley!" Elizabeth tried to cry. But the name sounded like gibberish, spoken into a smothering pillow. She tried to move, but her body wouldn't obey. She felt herself recede; flatten out; surrender all dimension.

All at once, Elizabeth understood—they weren't *sharing* this vision. The vision *belonged* to Sir Shanley. The man had been here so long, his mind now dominated this world. It was *his* chessboard, *his* furniture, *his* palace. Everyone else was a guest in *his* mind. Sir Shanley's imagination had fused with the fictional world. To uproot him now would tear that vision apart.

"*Elizabeth…*" Sir Shanley wheezed. He seemed to speak from far away—another room, another universe. "*Do you swear to seek the truth…*" His voice wavered in and out, like a poorly tuned radio. "*…to cherish and protect it… to redress wrongs… to seek justice… to further the peace and prosperity of mankind…*"

Elizabeth received the sentences one by one. She digested them in her mind, and all at once she shouted into the thickening abyss: "Yes! *Yes!*"

The room deteriorated. The floors and screens blurred, and the long table was smeared into the background. Every object melted into a fog of colors and forms. Elizabeth couldn't see the furniture's edges, the walls or ceiling. Every surface blended into the others. Nothing ended or began.

Then Elizabeth saw it—

—*the Somalodge.*

Her eyes trembled open, but not all the way. She looked through the reedy jumble of her own eyelashes. Elizabeth could make out Sir Shanley. The *real* Sir Shanley. His shrunken figure in the chair. His body shook. Dr. O'Malley grappled his neck from behind. Lexi loomed above them both. Plucking needles out of Sir Shanley's skin.

She closed her eyes. She clenched them shut. Elizabeth felt herself descend back into the dream, saw the washed-out shapes of Sir Shanley's palace, the orange sun burning in the distance. She turned her head, a slow and arduous movement

She saw Larimer.

Larimer gazed at her. His eyes were soft, deep. They weren't the eyes of a panther at all. They appraised her. Elizabeth opened her mouth, but Larimer speak first. A warbled voice flowed from his feline mouth. His lips barely moved. It wasn't sound so much as thought—syllables swimming from one mind to another.

"*Aykay,*" came the word. "*Aykay tayrahroom…*"

❖

Elizabeth's eyes flew open. She swallowed smoky air and gasped at the ceiling. She reached up and grabbed the needles in her head. They shocked her fingers, but she barely felt the electrical pain. Elizabeth the ripped needles out, two at a time. She heaved for breath.

Across the room, Sir Shanley writhed.

Elizabeth slid down the chair's cushions. Her limbs were useless. Her body was marmalade.

"*Aykay...*" she spluttered.

Dr. O'Malley looked up. His eyes focused on her.

"*Elizabeth!*" he shrieked. "*Elizabeth, are you all right?*"

"*Aykay   tayrahroom…*"   she   garbled   back.   "*Aykay tayrahroom...*"

One by one, the dreamers stirred. Elizabeth saw the bearded man in the riding boots, opening his eyes. The Indian couple shuddered; their fingers curled. The room was coming alive. Their vision was melting. The electrical currents fizzled in their wires. The figures reached for the needles. They looked around, trying to remember where they were—where they *really* were.

Elizabeth mumbled to herself. Her body was anchored to the chair. The room shifted and swayed before her. This place felt unreal—as unreal as the dream, as Sir Shanley's palace. For a long minute, Elizabeth did not belong to either world—real or imagined—but to both.

And with that thought, her head dropped forward, and everything went dark.

❖

"Easy does it," Dr. O'Malley said. He sat down beside Elizabeth, setting a cup of tea on her nightstand.

Elizabeth squinted into the morning light. Silver sunshine eased through the guestroom window. As her limbs stretched beneath the thick quilt, Elizabeth realized she was still wearing the same clothes. She wondered how she had come here; how long she'd slept; who had lay her here.

"How are you feeling?" Dr. O'Malley asked.

"Like a drowned cat," Elizabeth said. She yawned into the back of her hand.

All at once, she remembered. Emotion shot through her spine. She sat up in bed, tore the blanket aside. "Where is he? Where is Sir Shanley?"

"In his room," said Dr. O'Malley, laying his hand over hers.

"Is he… is he all right?"

"He's…" Dr. O'Malley licked his lips. "He *will* be all right."

Elizabeth turned sideways. Her legs dangled over the side of the mattress. She gazed into Dr. O'Malley's eyes. "He had a stroke, didn't he?"

"Yes."

"How bad?"

Dr. O'Malley grimaced. "It could have been a good deal worse."

Elizabeth's headed pounded. Her stomach felt empty. She yearned for breakfast, tea, a walk in the sunlight. She felt drained—but excitement still burbled beneath. She wanted to tell Dr. O'Malley everything—the dream, the palace, the chess match, Larimer, all of it. How had so much transpired in a single day? She started to slide off the bed, but Dr. O'Malley held out a hand.

"Before we join the others," he said slowly, "there's a matter to address."

"Oh?"

"What did you say, back in the Somalodge? Just before you fainted?"

"Please," Elizabeth recoiled. "Ladies in corsets *faint*. I like to think I *collapsed from exhaustion.*"

Dr. O'Malley leered impatiently.

"It was something I heard," Elizabeth said. "In the dream. There was a figure, there… he said, *Aykay tayrahroom.* Does that mean something?"

Dr. O'Malley nodded solemnly, then fiddled with one of his buttons. "It's Latin," he said. "*Ecce terrarum.*"

"Oh, for goodness sakes!" Elizabeth cried. "I should have known! That must mean… 'Behold, the world.'"

"Precisely." Dr. O'Malley adjusted his glasses. "If Sir Shanley said this to you, it means he holds you in great esteem."

"Me? Why?"

"I can't speak for him. And we must wait before he's well enough to speak. But I think diving headfirst into another man's dream—then trying to rescue him from his melancholy—did something to impress him."

Elizabeth smiled. "Well, that's what I always do on Thursday nights."

Dr. O'Malley didn't smile. He only stared at her intently.

"*Ecce terrarum* is what we say to welcome a new member." He held out a hand. "So, Elizabeth—welcome to the Order of Seshat."

SECOND LETTER

May, 1913

My Dearest Abner,

I suppose I should begin by squealing, "Happy New Year!" I may be five months tardy, but better late than never.

I should also bombard you with questions—how have you been? How is school? What are you dissecting these days? Have you found yourself a decent girl yet?

But I should also murmur an apology, and a late one, at that. I hope you'll forgive this long silence. Take heart: Not only haven't I forgotten about you, but I think about you all the time. *What will I tell Abner?* I think. *Would he even believe the things I've seen and done these past few months?* I am sworn to so much secrecy these days that I hardly want to whisper my own name. But each evening, I go back to my bedroom and see an old secretary desk. The pen and paper keep taunting me, even though I haven't had the first idea where to begin. So here I am tonight, forcing out the words, because I owe you that much. And anyway, who knows if you'll believe a jot of it?

To start: Dr. O'Malley took me to England, you'll recall, to a little town called Nestershire. Here I was supposed to meet a man named Sir Shanley, some sort of army veteran and (obviously) a knight, although that means a hill of beans to me.

I was supposed to confer with him about something important, something the professor couldn't yet tell me about. But as it happens, the two men had lost touch, in the weeks before I left. And when we showed up at his door, Sir Shanley had disappeared. His wife was there, but she's half-witted with dementia. She hadn't even noticed he was gone.

The full story is long and convoluted, and the particulars would make little sense to you. (It barely makes sense to me). But the short of it is this: Sir Shanley is alive and well, but he suffered a terrible stroke. He's been mostly bedridden, so I've taken up a room in his house—the very room in which I'm writing this letter, in fact.

So where have I been these six months? Locked away in an English mansion, feasting on its library.

Now, this is the important part, the part I'm not supposed to reveal to anyone. But it's so strange and delicious, I can't help but tell someone I trust. And since I hardly trust anyone, I've chosen you. But before you read another syllable, please, Abner, understand the gravity of my oath. You mustn't breathe a word of it to any soul, living or dead. Unless my letters are worth preserving for posterity, I hope you'll burn this very paper.

All right, here it is: I've joined a secret society of paranormal investigators.

It feels so good to put those words in writing. For the first time, my situation actually looks a bit like the fact that it is. I know this thing isn't much of a secret if I blab about it to friends, but nothing could be stranger than the truth. The secret society is quite real, and I am being groomed as its greenest member.

As you'll recall, I thought Dr. O'Malley was some kind of spy, but that's not the half of it. They call themselves the Order of Seshat. I recognized its namesake immediately—the ancient Egyptian scribe, a goddess who birthed history with her sacred stylus. Not as showy as Horus or Rah. Seshat is one of those gods nobody remembers, which seems like a fitting mascot for such a clandestine club.

Dr. O'Malley has told me a great deal. Their network is far-flung (more on that later), and I gather there are several leaders. But high up in the pantheon sits Sir Shanley. I wish I had met him earlier; he was such a gentleman, you can tell. But he's been hard to figure out. The same hour we met, he suffered that terrible stroke. He was bedridden for two weeks, prostrate and silent.

As for Dr. O'Malley, he's taken it upon himself to nurse Sir Shanley back to health. I can't tell whether he ever really practiced medicine, but I've been moved by Dr. O'Malley's bedside manner. He cares for the old man with the tenderness of a field nurse. He spoons soup to Sir Shanley's lips, monitors his pulse, and dutifully changes his bedpan. He's spent whole afternoons sitting nearby, watching him sleep. I doubt any son ever tended so lovingly to an ailing father.

Recovery is a slow and torturous thing, especially for a man so advanced in years. I'll spare you the grisly details, but it took nearly two months for Sir Shanley to become the man he is today—able to sit upright, yet paralyzed on one side, his left limbs useless. His shoulders slope diagonally, and half his face droops. One eye is sleepy, the other alert. He hasn't found his feet, and I doubt he ever will. But Dr. O'Malley pushes him through his mansion in a whicker wheelchair, and the right half of his body is downright spry.

❖

So what have *I* been doing all this time? How did I pass those two months of physical therapy? How have I passed the three months since?

Well, I did what I always do: I read books.

Each morning, Dr. O'Malley handed me a fresh title, which I devoured by suppertime. I moved from room to room; sprawled on the sofa; lay on my stomach in front of the fireplace; sat Indian-style on the stone bench outside. I have never read books so ravenously. The faded ink dances before me, seducing my eyes with every antiquated sentence. These were not the volumes you might find at your local bookshop, but dusty tomes as old as the printing press.

At the dinner table, Dr. O'Malley tests my memory—not in the bland way of examinations, but as a kind of Socratic dialogue.

One memorable evening, after I had read a book about Caribbean voodoo, he asked: "What did you think of the Haitian slave who was pronounced dead?"

And I responded: "It sounded far-fetched, that he'd come back to life and dig himself out of his grave."

Dr. O'Malley smiled at my dismissal, and we debated its credibility. For the first weeks, I clung to the truths I held dear—that animals cannot think, death is absolute, and no man can read another's mind. "How do you know?" Dr. O'Malley would ask. Or: "Can you truly disprove this account?" His contrarian stance infuriated me, like a child who asks "Why?" over and over, until your ration of answers is depleted. Question by question, Dr. O'Malley reduced my arguments to pudding. I could only combat one book with a different book, pit one authority against another, until, one fateful night, I threw up my hands and cried, "Well, what should I believe?"

Dr. O'Malley stood up. (You should have seen the twinkle in his eye). He straightened his dinner jacket and said, "Believe what you see. Believe a woman glided through the air. Believe you entered Sir Shanley's dreams. Your mates might call you daft, but learn to trust your senses. Science is the humblest discipline. A scientist must bow before his observations, no matter how his instincts might protest. The Order of Seshat was founded on this principle—believe the things you witness, never what you presume is true."

I couldn't sleep that night. Nothing has ever made so much sense to me. I doubted every fact I'd ever learned, and I delighted in that doubt. The simplest arithmetic felt flawed. By dawn, I wondered whether I could mix red and yellow paint and still get orange.

❖

When Sir Shanley was well enough, we pushed him outside in a wheelchair. He shivered in the February air, but the right side of his mouth curled into a smile. We wheeled him through the streets of Nestershire, through the central square and past the train station. Our destination was a narrow thoroughfare, nondescript except for a shoe-shop and old counting house. Sir Shanley is gaunt but tall, and Dr. O'Malley struggled to lug him up the staircase, to the second floor of an unmarked building. (I lifted him by the legs, but I doubt this did much good).

Imagine my surprise when we reached the top: The simple wooden door was covered in an iron gate, which Dr. O'Malley took pains to open. We finally stepped through the entrance, and there I saw it: The library of the Order of Seshat.

"Well, *one* library," corrected Dr. O'Malley.

"How many are there?" I asked.

"Six, in all. This is the smallest and most recent. Sir Shanley started it himself."

We whispered this exchange, not because there was anyone to listen, but out of sheer reverence. The chamber was small, and the stacks were packed tightly, leaving little walkways in-between. Each shelf sagged with volumes, and my index finger trembled before their spines.

"Go on," Dr. O'Malley said. "Take any one you like."

Here, Abner, I was surprised: The "books" were actually bound papers. Each page was a letter or document, written by hand or typed on a typewriter. I had no idea how they were organized, since they obeyed no library system I've ever used, and the gold lettering on their covers appeared encoded. I wish I could describe the sensation, flipping through that first book. Maybe this: I doubt I've ever really been in love, but this felt like a decent substitute.

There were two plush chairs, and Dr. O'Malley arranged them around Sir Shanley, so we could sit in a triangle. The room was frigid, so Dr. O'Malley dug out wool blankets and bundled us into them. He poured tea from a thermos, and we sipped, watching its steam curl in the still library air. I might have felt unnerved, the way Sir Shanley gazed at me with his one good eye, but I felt the opposite: He looked curious and proud. He looked like an art collector showing off a favorite painting, waiting for me to react.

Sir Shanley can barely speak, except in a thin murmur, and his speech is so slurred that I scarcely understand him. Dr. O'Malley has known the man since boyhood, and after so many weeks of care, only he could translate Sir Shanley's babble. For every sentence, Dr. O'Malley leaned in close, listened, nodded, and turned to me. Here is what Sir Shanley said:

"What you see, my dear, is thirty-two years of labor. When I purchased this building, in the spring of 1881, I intended to gather the secret knowledge of the world. This is our purpose—not only to study the uncanny, and intervene where necessary, but to document our findings. For every strange encounter, our investigators write a thorough report. Here you shall find writings, sketches, photographs, maps, tables—evidence and data that exist nowhere else on Earth. We receive the reports by post and cable, from every corner of the globe. We are masters of correspondence. We dedicate our lives to this research, and we would pay the ultimate price to keep these missives safe."

"But why?" I asked. "Why keep them secret?"

"Because," Dr. O'Malley said, "the truth is dangerous."

"Dangerous, how?"

"When the Order was founded," Dr. O'Malley said, "women were still drowned as witches. Heretics were burned at the stake. The clergy feared us. That time was terrible for science, as Galileo could attest. But now the consequences are more frightening. The world's full of tyrants and robber barons. Where some of us see threats, or villains, or victims in need, *they* might see opportunity."

"What do you mean? What kind of opportunity?"

"Kaiser Wilhelm wants a war," Dr. O'Malley said grimly. "Every king and czar and parliament in Europe is boiling with animosity. Suppose someone found Miss Greyson's formula. Suppose they injected a thousand soldiers with her serum. Suppose that army could levitate over enemy lines. What damage could those thousand soldiers wreak in a single night?"

I couldn't speak. Somehow that risk had never occurred to me. How awful, I thought, to corrupt such a wondrous discovery, and so easily.

"We must preserve this knowledge," Dr. O'Malley went on. "But we must conceal it as well. It is a delicate task. For us, there is no other way."

I couldn't resist any longer. The question had plagued me for months, and at last I blurted, "But why *me?*"

Dr. O'Malley glanced at Sir Shanley. The old Englishman closed his good eye, signaling permission.

"All told," Dr. O'Malley said slowly, "we have more than three hundred members. They are scattered across Europe and Asia. A handful live in Africa, a few in Australia. But the vast majority are here, in the European nations."

"So?"

"In all of the Americas, we have but two members."

"Two?" I exclaimed. "In the entire hemisphere?"

"Well—now only one." Dr. O'Malley grimaced. "The second one was me."

Sir Shanley piped up again. As he spoke his garbled speech, his body rocked back and forth. He looked more excited than before. Dr. O'Malley clapped his mentor on the shoulder and said, "We needed someone young. Someone sharp. Someone with a hunger for learning. And Elizabeth— the moment I met you, I could tell you were fearless. To us, you will not serve as a mere member, but as a pioneer. The Old World is well trod. But America? For us, it is *terra incognita*.

It is a book yet to be written. And you have your entire life ahead of you. If you take this torch, you will light the way for generations to come."

❖

I know all this is ridiculous. I feel like I've hoodwinked them. Me, of all people! For a bunch of scientists, they sure put a lot of faith in first impressions. I could be mad as a hatter, for all they know. I could sell them out for a pittance. Think of the headline: "FRIENDLESS GIRL EXPOSES RESEARCHER RING."

But they've got me. I know that. I couldn't wriggle away if I tried. For three months, I've spent every spare hour in that library, poring over reports. You would not believe the things I've learned—which is the point, I suppose. Imagine, that a Mongolian rock could raise the temperature of a room. Or a Stone Age tribe possesses skulls gilt in silver. Or that men have walked through walls without explanation. With every page I turn, my jaw hangs a little more open. Spoon-bending now seems plausible. Mythical creatures have apparently been spotted. And just when I want to laugh off the Abominable Snowman, I read an entry on yetis.

There's a reason I'm writing you now: I'm leaving this place soon. No one is more surprised than I. At dinner last night, Dr. O'Malley broke the news.

"You should pack your things," he said.

"Why?" I said through a mouthful of mutton.

"You're ready for the next phase of training."

"Oh? And what's that?"

I'd swear Dr. O'Malley hesitated. I think this news discomfited him. "Martial arts," he said. "You must learn to protect yourself."

I nearly jumped out of my skin. Martial arts? Protect myself? Could this really be happening? One day an archive, the next day an armory?

"And where will this *phase* be happening?"

"Santo Demetrio," he said.

"Is there a Santo Demetrio in England?"

"I'm afraid not. At the end of the week, you'll be headed to Spain.

And there you have it. Spain!

I'll forward the address as soon as I can. Pray for me, Abner. I don't put much stock in prayers, but they always sound more convincing in Hebrew. I'll write as soon as I can.

Sincerely Yours,

Liz

THE TERCENTENNIAL
SWORDSMAN

June, 1913

ELIZABETH TRUDGED UP the steep road. Her suede boots stumbled over yellow dust. She panted in the dry air, and her body ached from neck to toe. But she'd made progress: Before her loomed the windmill, its tower silhouetted against a blinding sun.

Almost there, she thought. *One foot in front of the other.*

The structure had taunted her for nearly two hours. After so many wrong turns on the garbled roads, so much doubling back, she was relieved to be so close. Elizabeth let the heavy knapsack slip from her shoulder and thump against the parched soil. She loosened the drawstrings just enough to dig out her field canteen and binoculars. After a sloppy swig, she turned around and gazed at the slope she had finally conquered.

The hills of Santo Demetrio curved gently into the vale, their bronzed fields lacerated with crumbled stone walls. Cork trees were scattered across the terrain, and warbled boughs waved lazily in the hot breeze. The town was only a hazy splotch of conjoined roofs, punctuated in the center with the high tower of its lone church. The only sound was the clang of cowbells as a distant herd of heifers meandered through their meadows.

When she spotted a dark V sailing through the sky, Elizabeth raised the binoculars to her eyes. The bird's rust-colored body was slung between two long wings, and the reddish hints betrayed its species.

"Red Kite," Elizabeth whispered to herself with satisfaction. *"Hola, mi amigo."*

She repacked her effects, took a thirsty breath, and resumed her walk, until she reached a rickety wooden door.

The windmill loomed above Elizabeth, taller and bulkier than she imagined. Time had stripped the whitewash from its surface, revealing the stonework underneath. The four sails were shattered; breeze seeped through the idle wreckage.

Attached to the tower was a high wall; the primitive masonry enclose a large yard. The double doors dangled open, barely sustained by their corroded hinges. Elizabeth might have walked right in, were it not for the boy.

The boy was a teenager, skinny as a toothpick. He reclined along the wall with romanesque indifference. His trousers were rolled up to his knee, and his flaxen shirt was clearly inherited from a larger man. His dark hair was curled and stiff, and he nodded to Elizabeth.

"*Buenas tardes*," he said.

"*Yo busco...*" Elizabeth closed her eyes, suddenly forgetting the name. "*Señor... señor...*"

"Sándor?" the boy smirked.

"Yes," Elizabeth sighed. "I mean, *sí.*"

The sleepy youth rose to his feet. He stretched his arms and let them swing at his sides. As he slouched through the doorway, Elizabeth watched the boy suppress a yawn.

The yard looked like an old fort: Decayed awnings extended from the walls; barrels and crates were stacked underneath. A lonely wagon slumped in the middle of the field, its belly full of burlap sacks. The place seemed abandoned, except for the man standing on the far end of the yard.

"Señor Sándor," announced the boy. He pointed, bowed, and back away, toward the door.

Elizabeth stopped a few paces from the man. She watched him splash water over his head and hair. The man leaned over a stone trough, which had long ago been used for livestock. The man's trousers were stuffed into his black boots; his gray work shirt was stained with sweat. Even the straps of his suspenders drooped from his waist.

"*Perdóname*," Elizabeth called out.

The man's movements slowed. He reached for a ragged towel and dried his hands. He was slim as a jockey, but his shoulders swelled like bocce balls around pronounced vertebrae. He turned his head halfway, revealing a sharp profile—an aquiline nose, a rugged jaw, and dry lips that curved conspiringly. But it was his eyes that disarmed her: Elizabeth had never seen such a shade of hazel, like a ball of orange fire wreathed in green. Even from a distance, those irises were overpowering. Elizabeth lingered there, speechless, her knapsack threatening to fall from her shoulder. The man leaned against the trough, crossed his meaty arms, and said, "So, you are Elizabeth."

His voice rumbled from a powerful chest, and Elizabeth barely recognized her own name: *Ay-leez-a-bet*.

"That's right," she said, lowering the bag. She adjusted her blouse, and—not knowing what to do with herself—crossed her own arms. "And you are Sándor."

The man nodded. Then, in one fluid movement, Sándor tossed the towel away, pushed off the trough, and sauntered toward her. He groped his suspender straps and drew them over his shoulders. His chestnut hair jumbled playfully around his face. His scruff was perfectly unshaven. Sándor moved with balletic ease, and when he stopped before Elizabeth, his dimpled chin nearly touched her forehead.

"They tell me you are brave," Sándor intoned.

Elizabeth could feel his breath on her brow. She struggled to ignore the piquant aroma of his glistening body.

"Should I be?" she said, trying not to stammer.

Sánder hovered there a moment, then pivoted on his heel. He strode over to the awning, where a table stood in the shadows. Elizabeth hadn't noticed it, perhaps because its surface was covered in a dark blanket. Sándor whipped the fabric away from the table, revealing a dozen metal shafts. Elizabeth forced herself to approach, and as her vision adjusted to the shade, she saw that they were knives. Each blade stood out from the others—long and skinny, short and fat, some sheathed, some naked, all of them deadly sharp.

Eyes half-open, Sándor meditated by the table, his finger drawing an invisible line across the collection.

"You are small," declared Sándor. "You are light. If a man carries *this*—" Sándor snatched a blade from the table. He held it by the knifepoint, then flipped it in the air, catching the weapon by its hilt. The edge glinted menacingly as Sándor stepped back into the sun. "—it will not matter how brave you are. You must know how to protect yourself."

"Well," said Elizabeth. "That's why I'm here, isn't it?"

Sándor smirked. His head bobbed to a contemplative rhythm. He took a couple of steps toward Elizabeth, the knife hanging loosely from his digits.

"Hit me," he said.

Elizabeth furrowed her brow. "*Hit* you?"

"Yes."

"Where?"

Sándor shrugged. "Wherever you pref—"

Elizabeth hit him.

How natural it felt. She reared back, squeezed her fingers tight, and let the fist fly. She felt her knuckles slam into that leathery cheek, and Sándor's head cocked sideways. He took a step back, bounced on his feet, and released a powerful laugh.

"*Good!*" he cried. "*Very good!*"

Elizabeth reeled. She hadn't thrown a punch since the schoolyard, and a wave of pain and elation shot through her. An ache swelled in the joints of her hand. She felt heady and strange.

Sándor's laugh dissipated. His expression hardened.

"However," he said, "you must be careful."

The man stepped toward her. Sándor grappled her wrist and raised it to her face. Elizabeth felt her body petrify. The movement was swift. Elizabeth didn't even gasp; she watched her own hand appear at eye-level, clenched by the stranger. The grip was ironclad; one good jerk could snap her radius like a twig.

"You must never form a fist around your thumb," Sándor said. "Your thumb must remain *outside* the fist, or else you shall break it." He lowered his head. His eyes penetrated her. "You understand?"

Elizabeth felt herself nod.

And just like that, Sándor released her wrist and whirled away. He laid the knife gently alongside the others. Then he spread his arms across the shaded table and leaned into them.

"You have traveled far," said Sándor. "And now we have met. Go back to your flat. Rest. Clear your mind. Tomorrow we begin in earnest."

❖

Elizabeth collapsed into her chair—and groaned. Her body felt brittle and bruised, and she regretted spending so many months in the library, allowing herself to atrophy. She had been such an active youth, running around the neighborhood, climbing trees, playing hopscotch. Few other children ever joined her, but she never cared. Yes, she devoured books and always had, but all this sitting around had ruined her. She imagined her muscles dissolving into lard.

Elizabeth scanned the apartment with drowsy eyes. It wasn't much: a humble room, a lonely bed, a writing desk, and this stiff little chair. Against the wall leaned a long sheet of glass, which served as her mirror. A wooden cross was nailed to the plaster.

The landlady was named Doña Segarra, an old woman with woolen hair and a bitterly wrinkled face. Elizabeth had met her briefly, when she arrived three days before. All she had received from Doña Segarra was a rusty key and a litany of house rules—spoken in a broken monologue of English and Catalan. The boarding house had two other apartments, but they appeared to be vacant. She doubted that anyone holidayed in Santo Demetrio, and this crumbling old *casa* wasn't exactly the Ritz.

Elizabeth gazed out the window at the street below, where women in dark dresses ambled past, lugging baskets down the cobbled pavement. The cream-colored buildings were crammed together; their balconies jutted from the old stonework. Most of these façades were houses; Elizabeth imagined their interiors, doubting she'd ever step inside. Her street had only one shop; the carved wood sign above the door read "*Botica*," which meant apothecary, according to her dog-eared Spanish phrasebook. The sun was low, and long shadows cast everything in violet; yet the maze of terracotta roofs still glowed with solar light. Pigeons cooed and trotted along the gutters, and now and again she heard the mewl of a stray cat.

Elizabeth reached deep into her knapsack. She pulled a bag into the dusty air—a leather pouch. She yanked it open and plucked out a delicate piece of paper. Then she pinched some green nuggets out of the darkness. She crumpled the dry leaves and spread them across the paper. She did this studiously, exactly as Mr. Fung had taught her. Then she rolled the paper between her fingertips, licked the end, and sealed the marijuana cigarette with a twist.

She examined her work approvingly. She liked this new pastime—the only thing she'd hidden from Professor O'Malley, all those long winter months. She fumbled for her matchbox and lit a flame. Pungent smoke swirled out of the reefer, and she swallowed its earthy flavor. When she finally exhaled, the smoke poured out of her. She forgot about the day's exhaustion; the long hike up the hill; the bored young Spaniard.

Instead, she thought of Sándor.

Who *was* he? All she knew was his name. His features could pass for Spanish, but his accent wasn't any kind of Spanish. Sir Shanley had told her little, only that she should travel alone to Spain, arrive in the town of Santo Demetrio, and meet Sándor at *el molino viejo*—the old windmill—on a hill above town. Everything had gone according to plan. She had easily checked into this boarding house, where Doña Segarra had stoically greeted her, and the rent was already paid.

Elizabeth stubbed her roach into the windowsill. Her mind swirled with a thousand thoughts. But one thing superseded them all: the memory of Sándor's hand around her wrist. That moment of contact had stirred her. The sensation she had felt was not fear, but warmth, *elation*. She had never stood so close to a man—not that she could remember, anyhow. So many senses had awakened in that moment—the sight of him, the scent of him, his tigerish voice. And then his *touch*, as clinching as a manacle.

Yet she hadn't been afraid. Despite his grip, his knife, his stoic words, there was something else. A *presence*. It comforted her.

But why? Why should this stranger, this trained killer, put her so at ease? Was it Sir Shanley's assurances? Was it her faith in the Order? Or was it Sándor himself—his cool demeanor, his quiet confidence—that made her feel safe?

No, *more* than safe. What was this feeling?

"Alive," she thought. A moment passed before she realized she'd said the word aloud. She guffawed at this, then flung herself on the bed, giggling in the empty room.

❖

The next morning, just as Elizabeth stepped into the yard, Sándor was holding a sword.

Outside a museum, Elizabeth had only seen one sword in her life—her grandfather's cavalry saber, a curved blade with a faded gold hilt. Her mother had brought it down from the attic one day, though Elizabeth couldn't remember why. The sword was dull and bent, a precious tool that had moldered in a chest.

Sándor faced away from Elizabeth. He stood sideways, his knees bent. One hand was pressed against his hip, while the other held the weapon—a rapier, long and slim. A tiny round plate protected his hand. He moved slowly, putting one front foot forward, then the rear foot. Advancing across the dusty grass, he reminded Elizabeth of a cat stalking its prey, those final methodical steps before it pounced.

Then Sándor *lunged*—he launched himself forward. His body straightened diagonally. The sword point struck the stone wall. The blade bent. He froze there for a moment. The arc of the weapon so severe that Elizabeth thought it might snap. He retreated from the wall, and the sword resumed its shape. Sándor ran his fingers across his scalp. He swished the sword through the air.

"You are early," he said.

Elizabeth started. She hadn't made a sound, nor had Sándor turned around to see her. But she decided not to acknowledge this. Instead she cleared her throat. "I'm nothing if not punctual."

Sándor turned around. He smiled. His eyes were downturned. Without fanfare, he chucked the sword at the ground; the point stuck fast in the soil, and the blade wavered in the air. Sándor's gloved hands grasped his thick belt. With his white tunic and black pantaloons tucked into his boots, he looked like a Slavic dancer.

Sándor pointed at her with a limp hand. "You are dressed for sport," he said.

Elizabeth grimaced. She wore a thick cotton skirt; its pleated cloth was divided down the middle, like trousers. She had commissioned her leather boots from a London shoemaker; the tan blouse was tailored for safaris. Her hair was bound with a coarse kerchief. The garments were tough and durable. She felt her chest puff with poise.

"I'm nothing if not prepared," Elizabeth leered. "Except punctual, of course."

"Let me ask you," said Sándor, raising a finger to his nose. "Suppose you were invited to the symphony. Would you wear—*this?*"

Elizabeth licked her lips. "Fancy dress has never been my strong suit."

"In a classroom, then," Sándor said. "Are these the vestments you would choose?"

"I wear what I like in the classroom," Elizabeth shot back. "That's one nice thing about nobody ever noticing you."

"Even so," said Sándor sternly, "a killer waits for nothing. When he ambushes you, you have no time to change your clothing. Here, you must learn to protect yourself—in any place, at any time. In *any apparel*."

Elizabeth felt a surge of feeling. Her mouth tightened. Her eyes quivered in their sockets. She clenched her fingers—though she was careful not to enclose her thumb.

"Maybe I should come in my nightgown," she growled. "Since I spend a third of my life in it."

She hoped that Sándor would redden, or recoil, or brush her off. But he was unmoved. "Perhaps you should," he replied.

Elizabeth jutted her chin. "You'd like that, wouldn't you?"

A trace of a smile. "Perhaps I would," Sándor murmured.

Elizabeth couldn't think of a response. Her mouth opened and closed.

Sándor whirled away from Elizabeth. He returned to the table—the one in the shade. He grasped the edge of a black sheet and peeled it back. Elizabeth expected the same row of knives, but they had been replaced: There, dark and heavy, lay a row of pistols.

"My God..." Elizabeth breathed.

"A firearm," Sándor declared, "is the weapon of a coward. A pistol needs no skill, no *art*. You may kill your opponent from a hundred paces. Any fool may wield its power. Sadly, the world is full of such cowards. This is the reason you must learn its use."

The lesson began in a mechanical way: Sándor handed Elizabeth a weapon, opened its cylinder, and inserted a handful of bullets. He showed her how to hold it, how to cock the hammer, how to aim. He named each of them—the Browning M1900, the Colt M1892, the Smith & Wesson No. 3—and he pointed to their barrels, slides, front sites, recoil shields, and trigger guards. He slammed cartridges into grips, then removed them so that Elizabeth could try. Never had Elizabeth appreciated the weapons' heft or design, and she silently studied the munitions that rotated through her hands. She listened, committing each name to memory.

"Now," said Sándor. "Pick one."

Elizabeth surveyed the guns. The familiar six-shooters. The more clinical automatics. She felt herself reaching for one. Then, convinced, she picked it up. It was the strangest-looking contraption of all, with a square body and narrow barrel.

"Ah," said Sándor. "The Mauser C96. You have unusual taste."

"You're hardly the first to say so," Elizabeth retorted. "So—pistols at dawn?"

Sándor did not dignify her quip. Instead, he went to the corner of the yard. He spent some minutes dragging wood stumps, then spreading them out along the wall. Satisfied with their placement, he turned to a satchel, which hung from a nail. He drew three wine bottles into the light. He examined them studiously, then gathered them in his arms and approached the stumps. Elizabeth squinted with surprise; the bottles were dark and heavy in his hands. She realized they were full.

As Sándor positioned the bottles for target practice, Elizabeth felt her pulse quicken. She took deep breaths, but they failed to ease her nerves.

"Say, aren't those bottles supposed to be empty?"

Sándor nodded. He gestured to one of the printed labels. "Austrian wine," he said. "It is unworthy of human consumption."

"*Hungarian!*" Elizabeth blurted. "You're Hungarian, aren't you?"

Sándor retained the same cryptic smile. He set down the final wine bottle and stepped away from the stump.

"From where you are standing," he commanded, "take aim. And fire at will."

Elizabeth raised the Mauser. It felt heavy, as if the steel had suddenly reverted into wrought iron. She watched that shaft of metal vibrate in her hand; her fingers were clenched so tight that her knuckles burned white.

"See the bottle," Sándor murmured. "Focus…"

"*Ssh!*" Elizabeth scowled.

Her finger embraced the trigger, but she could not summon the strength to pull it. Her fingernail tapped nervously against the trigger ring. She feared what would happen next—the sound, the kickback. She squeezed, but the little eyelash wouldn't budge. At last she clenched her teeth, crinkled her nose, and flexed her finger—

—the gun exploded. Smoke blew out of every crevice. Pain shot through the bones of her hand. Her ears buzzed, and she felt faint. A haze dissipated before her eyes.

The line of bottles remained, undisturbed. Even the plaster wall behind them looked untouched. The bullet had vanished into thin air.

ROBERT ISENBERG

"God*damn* it!" Elizabeth wailed, nursing her throbbing palm.

"Again!" Sándor commanded.

"Just a goddamned *second*."

"No! *Again!*"

Elizabeth glowered, but she lifted the gun again. Sparks flew as the shots rang out, five rounds in succession. A scream burbled up inside her, dying to escape through her gullet, but Elizabeth refused to cry out.

When the fog of burnt gunpowder lifted, the bottles still stood, as defiant as ever.

"Again!" called Sándor.

Elizabeth hurled the pistol at the ground. "No," she pouted. "There's no point."

Sándor's eyes blazed. He smacked his hands together, but Elizabeth could barely hear their clap over the ringing in her ears.

"*Again! Again!*"

"Damn it, Sándor, I *can't*. You're wasting both our time."

"Practice!" he commanded. "Practice, practice!"

"Sándor," growled Elizabeth, "I'm *not coordinated*, all right? I might as well shoot cross-eyed. I can waste your bullets all you want. But at the end of the day, those bottles will sooner shoot me."

Sándor puffed out his lips. "Elizabeth, you will do as I instruct."

"Or what? I won't learn how to miss the broad side of a barn? *I can't do it*, Sándor. And I certainly can't do it wearing a bathrobe, or whatever it is you think I wear out."

Sándor cocked an eyebrow, then his head. "You *can* do this."

"And how would you know?" Elizabeth snapped. "You don't know a thing about me. *I* happen to know a great number of things about me—I can't throw a baseball, I can't hit a dart board, and I *cannot shoot a gun.*"

Sándor looked away. Embarrassed, perhaps. Unequipped to answer such a tantrum. She stood there, ears still ringing. As the silence grew, so did her doubt. Suddenly, she *wanted* to hear his commands. Not because she wanted to try again, but to fill the vacuum. She couldn't guess what he was thinking, now. She sensed disappointment. But wasn't *she* disappointed? To crack so easily? Was this all she expected of herself? To succumb so quickly to shame?

"Go back," said Sándor. "That is enough for today."

Elizabeth rocked on her feet. Was this what she wanted? To be dismissed? Did she want him to accept her failure?

It was too late to save face, she knew. She turned toward the gate.

"Wait," Sándor said.

She stopped. She looked. She waited for a sign—a nod, a good word, anything.

"Leave the gun," he snapped. "For heaven's sake."

❖

Elizabeth was in the middle of dinner when she first heard the bells.

Evening meals were a rare excuse to leave her room. Each of the past four evenings, Doña Segarra has opened a cauldron and ladled its contents into a bowl, coupled with a whole baguette. Gazpacho was new to Elizabeth, and she had frowned at the notion of cold soup, but the beans and tomatoes won her over. Now she looked forward to the dish that had seemed so penal; tonight she came with an appetite. She looked forward to that dark dining room and its rotted wood table.

As Elizabeth devoured her last heel of bread, she heard the clang. They were church bells, coming from the stone tower in the middle of town. She recognized the deep resonance that announced each hour. But this was different; the ringing went on, insistent. Elizabeth set down her spoon and went to the front door. The bell tolled faster. An announcement. An alarm.

Doña Segarra was already standing in the street. She wore her usual black *stola*, and she hugged her tight-wrapped shawl. She scowled at the distant tower.

"*Que pasa, Señora?*" asked Elizabeth.

"*El desafío,*" she muttered. But that was all. The Señora raised a fist, shook her head, and pushed past Elizabeth, back into the house.

People walked past. They shuffled down the block, toward the sound. Elizabeth followed them—a few men, a few women. Then more—dozens, scores, clumping together in the narrow streets. Elizabeth saw the town in all its diversity; old men; the housewives; youths and children careening past elbows. Cooks in aprons; sun-bronzed laborers; farmers and maids. Some were familiar; Elizabeth spotted the cockeyed pharmacist who tended shop across the street; the balding baker who sold magdalenas from a window; the cherubic friar who always swept the church steps. The crowd swallowed her up, and Elizabeth followed the human tide deeper into town, until they arrived at the central plaza.

The square was wide and paved with stones. A plain fountain, which had long run dry, stood in the middle. The open space was ringed with shops and houses. A basilica church stood in the center. The sun hovered blindingly over the bell tower; the frantic rings pained her eardrums. Elizabeth maneuvered through the throng, dodging limbs and slipping between shoulders. She found herself at the fore, where a group of boys were sitting pretzel-style on the ground.

In the center, there was an empty space. Outlined in a dense human wall.

Near Elizabeth, a man stood. He was a young, perhaps twenty-five, with a long and slender frame. He was dressed in a shimmering red shirt, its middle bound in a thick belt. His trousers were black wool, stuffed into calf-girdling boots. At his side dangled a sword; his hand rested on its serpentine hilt. The blade was needle-like within its leather sheath. The young man had a high and narrow face; his head was nearly shaved around the ears and occipital, accenting the oily thickness of his parted hair. Most impressive was his Adam's apple, which protruded from his skinny neck, like a prow.

On the far side, another man faced him. This man was older, but no less virile. He was compact, clothed in a simple gray tunic. His naked scalp glistened in the sun; his forehead rippled fiercely. His face was dark with shadows; he reminded Elizabeth of a sea turtle. A salt-and-pepper beard outlined his iron jaw, and he glared through slitted eyes.

The bells stopped. The silence was abrupt. All Elizabeth could hear were scattered coughs, the shift of feet.

The Young Man moved first. He ripped the sword from his side, then slashed the air with an audible *whisk*. His spidery legs stepped purposefully, toes touching first, like a ballerino. He made a slow arc, then countered the other way.

His opponent only watched. His body still at rest. He blinked slowly. He watched the Young Man approach, hands clasped over his waist.

Then, in an instant, the sword shot out. The Elder Man didn't put himself en garde. He didn't fall into the fencer's stance—legs bent, free arm hanging behind. The Elder Man only aimed the swordpoint at his enemy. Aimed it like a spear. He stared down that length of steel, directly into the other's eyes.

The Young Man stopped. *Everything* stopped. No breath was taken. Elizabeth's throat caught. The outcome was already clear—as clear as those nefarious eyes. One of these men would die. And there was no question which man it would be.

Elizabeth had seen sword fights dramatized—the requisite Shakespeare plays of her youth—and only now did she realize how wrong they were. The two men moved quickly, keeping distance, like two opposed magnets. The weapons guided their bodies, slicing viciously through the yellow air, yet refused to meet. Elizabeth waited for the clang of metal, the jaunty repartee; yet these were not the musketeers of novels. The edges shimmered, razors thirsting to cut.

The Young Man moved first. He lunged, but the Elder Man stepped back. Blades flicked against each other—not to combat, but to strike fear. The Elder Man stepped slowly, a coiled viper. And then—*he sprang*.

The Young Man retreated, but his long legs bundled together. He lost his balance. He leaned into his back leg. That was all it took.

The Elder Man knocked the skinny sword away. His blade sank deep. It eased between the Young Man's ribs, passing underneath the shoulder blade. Blood seeped darkly through the crimson fabric.

The crowd erupted in gasps and wails.

The Elder Man let go of his sword. He sauntered away, dismissive.

The Young Man stepped back, impaled, the sword rising and falling with every futile breath. He swallowed; his pronounced throat throbbed. He dropped his sword, and it clattered on the paving stones. The Young Man fell to his knees, sputtering blood. He let himself crumple sideways, fondling the instrument of his demise.

The masses converged around him. They devoured the dying man in heads and shoulders. Elizabeth was paralyzed; she felt the rush of townsfolk clamoring past her.

All at once, she remembered Miss Greyson's face, the moment she was struck. The shock. The frozen disbelief. Elizabeth had seen dozens of cadavers, dissected them on tables. But the dance of death was something different.

Now she understood. *This* was what Sándor was preparing her for—a world where things like this could happen, and the certainty of life could drain away, leaving behind only the panic of survivors.

❖

Elizabeth dragged herself to the front gate. She paused, feeling her shoulders collapse into her aching sternum. She could scarcely look at the battered door without tasting bile.

Yet there it was, open and beckoning. The boy was gone; somehow his absence accented her dread. Her boots were glued to the hard earth, and she could barely muster another step.

"I'm doing this for you, Professor," she whispered to herself. "This better be worth it."

But when she stepped into the courtyard, her nose crinkled with surprise. There, on the middle of the lawn, stood two horses.

Sándor stood between them, their reins bunched in a single leather glove. His free hand stroked their faces, a loving touch. Sándor gazed into the horses' black eyes, running fingers through their manes. Both animals were powerfully built, their black hair glistening like oil in the morning sun.

Elizabeth came closer, but Sándor said nothing. Instead, he stretched the reins in her direction.

Elizabeth took the leather straps and approached the handsome creatures. The stallions bowed to her hand; their hair bristled between her fingers. Elizabeth cocked her head sideways to examine his tack—a tough and weighty saddle. There was nothing dainty about these animals. This kind of horse was bred for long rides.

"There is a chapel," said Sándor, brusquely. "La Capella de San Lorenzo. It stands two miles from here. You must ride to it."

"Oh?" murmured Elizabeth, still transfixed by the horses. "What will I find there?"

"Nothing," said Sándor. "But you must reach it before I do."

Elizabeth stiffened. "Or else what?"

Sándor stepped into a stirrup. Swiftly, he propelled his body over his horse's back. "Or else I will send you back to London. And you shall never be welcome here again."

Elizabeth's lips curled. Her body hardened like an eggshell. In one fluid motion, she lifted herself onto the saddle. She fit her toes into the unfamiliar stirrups and pulled gently on the reins.

"Which way?"

"North," said Sándor.

North. Elizabeth patted the horse's neck. She felt the sun beating on her back. *That's coming from the east*, she thought. *I'm facing west. South is to my left. To my right—north.*

"You are ready?" Sándor demanded.

Elizabeth didn't answer.

She jammed her feet into the horse's haunches. The animal launched forward, thumping its shoes into the dust.

Warm breeze eased through her hair. Elizabeth scarcely noticed her hat falling from her head, saved only by the string that entwined her neck. She reached the door and bounded into the open air. The valley emerged in all its hazy splendor.

She heard Sándor. Riding behind her. Hard and fast. She felt so airy and light, compared to that awful gallop. Elizabeth crouched forward, pressing her belly into the stallion's spine.

For a split-second, she thought to slow down, to let Sándor fly ahead, so she could use his direction as a guide. But the land was so empty. Surely she could find the chapel herself. And why give that brute the satisfaction? She must press on, ahead of Sándor. She must track the chapel herself.

A stone wall threatened her way. She gritted her teeth, clung to the reins, and felt the stallion leap into the air. The hooves crashed into gravel road. The horse skidded, but they stayed upright, leaning into the turn.

Two miles. Elizabeth's mind raced, matching the pace of the horse's frantic footfalls. The building would be small, surely. Stone, perhaps. She should look for a small steeple; a cross.

The ground scrolled beneath her, an abstraction of yellow and gray. She squinted at the terrain beyond, two hemispheres of land and sky. On one side, a jagged stone wall; on the other, open meadow.

Elizabeth heard movement behind her. Sándor, closing in. She sensed his bulk, his power, his predation. But she pushed it out of her mind. There was only the road ahead. Relentless forward progress.

A shape pierced the skyline. A peaked roof. A cross. Beyond the scattered trees; up the grassy slope. The chapel grew; its plain walls emerged beneath the roof.

The horse was slowing. Elizabeth felt its fatigue. She had ridden the animal hard. Sándor was gaining, she knew.

But he's still behind me, she thought. *I can still win.*

The stallion whinnied. The chapel was large now. Elizabeth saw a small yard, a wooden fence. She threw herself from the horse, landing gracelessly on the ground. She sprinted toward the gate, arms outstretched.

A shadow fell over her. A gloved hand clapped her shoulder. She felt hot breath on her nape.

Elizabeth swiveled. She rammed her palm into flesh and bone. Sándor recoiled, his jaw knocked sideways.

She didn't even pause. Elizabeth hurled herself against the chapel's door. She felt her forehead bang into the wood. Pain shocked through her skull. She was weightless. Her arms spread wide as she ricocheted from the door, sprawling across the soil.

And there she lay.

Everything was still. Slowly, her brain stopped spinning. Elizabeth looked up at a sky smudged with clouds. Her chest heaved. Her shoulders settled into the dirt. Her pulse pounded in her temples. She sensed the welt forming above her eye. Yet she also felt a rush of elation. *I touched the door*, she thought. *I got here first.*

Sándor chuckled. But it was a low chuckle, humble and pensive. His boots crunched in the grass, and then he squatted low.

Sándor rubbed his face; his scruffy cheek was rosy where Elizabeth had smacked him.

"You ride well," he said.

Elizabeth sat up. She groaned quietly, and the ache ballooned in her forehead.

"You can't deny," huffed Elizabeth, "that you let me win. You're right—I ride well. I've ridden horses since I was a girl. But I'm no match for a Hungarian."

Sándor gazed solemnly at the gate. "You are a bad shot," he said. "And you do not like guns. These are handicaps, in the field. You *must* know these weapons."

Elizabeth sighed bitterly. "Whatever you say."

"*Yet,*" continued Sándor, "a warrior must know her strengths. How she excels. You will never be a great marksman. This much is clear. But as a rider..." He nodded coolly. "Today, you have tasted victory. You must remember this feeling. You must know that, yes, you have bested even a Magyar."

Elizabeth couldn't help but grin. She sat silently, relishing the morning sun. Was he lying? Did it matter? The man had sacrificed his pride for her morale. How many men would stoop to this? How many men would give her a chance at all?

"Your body will never be strong," mused Sándor. "You will never be quick. You are small and clumsy. But you are also clever. And you will fight to the end. These are your strengths. If you cannot overpower your enemy, you must *surprise* him."

Sándor stood up and brushed the straw from his breeches. "Tomorrow, you must find a way to surprise me. That is your assignment."

He strode toward the edge of the gate, where their stallions grazed.

"What about the horse?" croaked Elizabeth.

"For as long as you are in Spain," called Sándor over his shoulder, "he is yours."

❖

The shop was small, but dense with stock. Shelves lined the walls, each supporting dozens of colored bottles. Elizabeth nodded to the man at the counter, a rolly polly fellow with a receding hairline. He nodded back, and whispered, "Señora."

Tags dangled from each bottle, but the handwritten names confounded her. Elizabeth had puzzled out some Spanish, and she had forced her way through conversations. But these names meant nothing to her; pharmaceuticals were beyond the pages her phrase book, and she handled each piece of cardboard with indifference.

This is going nowhere, she thought. *I just have to ask.*

She turned to the man. She stretched her arms across the counter and looked at him squarely. "*Tengo una situación especial*," she said. "*Yo busco un veneno.*"

The man breathed deeply. He looked both ways. He ran fingers through his remaining patches of hair. "*Vale.*"

"*Pero*," added Elizabeth, "*no quiero matar el hombre. Solo paralizarlo.*"

The man changed. He looked up, thinking. And then, as if seeing her for the first time, he nodded. "*Tengo exactamente lo que necesita.*"

Elizabeth smirked. The man understood. And for the first time in her life, Elizabeth wanted to learn every language on earth.

❖

Sándor sat on a stump, sharpening his sword with his whet stone. He focused on the ribbon of steel, drawing the stone meditatively along its blade. He paused to blow across its surface, then polished the already gleaming metal with a white cotton rag.

On the ground, two carpets were sprawled. Long ago, they had been colorful and neatly patterned. Now the carpets had faded; the weaving was clotted with dust. The edges curled at opposite ends, and they were lumpy in the middle, signifying years of storage.

"Swords again?" Elizabeth asked, still breathy from the long hike. "Or are we beating rugs today?"

"Wrestling," Sandor said.

Elizabeth tried not to smile. She dreaded this response. She had never once seen her high school wrestling team in action, despite their decent record, and she knew nothing of the sport. Yet she was amused by the way Sándor said the word. The man spoke such impeccable English; Elizabeth no longer acknowledged his trilled R's and oddly shaped vowels. Yet *wrestling* was a tricky word for the Hungarian to master. At first Elizabeth thought he said *riesling*, and imagined them on a picnic.

"Before we get to the fisticuffs," said Elizabeth dryly, "could I have a sip of your water?"

Sándor nodded unpleasantly. "Yes. Go. You ought to drink more water, anyway."

Elizabeth found the trough in the corner. She saw it up close for the first time; a long, cement sink, lined with rough masonry. The terracotta pitcher stood on one end, a stain of dried water running from its pouted lip. Elizabeth pulled down on the rusted metal lever, and the old pump squealed miserably. At last, glistening water trickled from the spout. Elizabeth cupped her fingers and slurped. Then, as casually as she could, she unsnapped her satchel and slipped a hand inside.

She turned her head—ever so slightly.

Sándor remained distant, turned away.

Elizabeth wiped her chin dramatically. She returned to the carpet, stretching, one arm after the other. Sándor was still seated, but he was now removing his boots, a cumbersome task. The boots clung tightly to his calves, and he struggled to free them from the curve of his ankle. He ripped off his socks as well, and Elizabeth took her cue: She stepped out of her boots and felt the scraggly grass beneath her bare feet.

"You know how strike with your fist," Sándor said. "You have proven this. Your strength is deceptive. This is an asset to you. Yet a large man is powerful. He will overwhelm you with his body. You must anticipate his movements. You must outsmart him."

Sándor bent his knees. He hunched over, and his arms turned into hooks. Elizabeth aped his posture; to her surprise, the stance felt natural, as if she had struck this pose a hundred times before.

"If I move like this, what do you do?" As he spoke, Sándor reached out with his hand, touching Elizabeth's forearm. She cheated sideways, pulling her elbow into herself.

"Good," said Sándor. "In hand-to-hand combat, your feet are your most dangerous weapons. If you control the distance between us, you decide when to strike, as well."

They moved. Their hands met, then pulled back. Sándor reached, slowly, for her knee, and she stepped away. Elizabeth felt herself circle around him, avoiding every reach.

"The woman must use a man's power against him," mused Sándor. "He is heavy. Slow. You are light, like the breeze. This is the only way to defeat him."

He moved faster. A swipe. A sudden lunge. Elizabeth bounced away, breathing hard.

"But you must be aware," said Sándor, his voice darkening. "There is one weakness nearly every woman has."

He stepped forward. His hand emerged behind her head. His fingers twisted through her hair. He clinched, and Elizabeth's head fell back. As Sándor tugged at her hair, Elizabeth felt pain—in her scalp, in her strained neck, in her bending back. Her eyes blurred with tears. The skin burned; she felt follicles uproot. Sándor's chest pressed into her bosom; the malevolent muscles tensed against her. The tips of their noses nearly touched.

"This is the act of a cowardly man," seethed Sándor. "The cruel husband. The drunken sailor. The pain you feel— it is a man's hatred for a woman. It should never be done. But men will resort to this. They will use a woman's beauty against her. Here, there is one way to stop a man—you must use his manhood against him." He narrowed his eyes. "Do it now."

Slowly, through the delirium of pain, Elizabeth realized what Sándor meant. She imagined lifting her foot. She could kick him squarely between the legs. This was her chance. This was his command. One kick, and all this pain would end.

But she didn't move. She whimpered, struggled, but her feet stayed put.

"Do it!" cried Sándor.

"You've… made your… point," squeaked Elizabeth.

"*Do it now.*"

"I don't… *feel* like it," Elizabeth snarled.

Sándor let go. But even the release was painful; the sweat-soaked hair stuck to his fingers, and he struggled to untangle himself. Elizabeth fell to her knees, groping her swollen head.

"Will you *feel like it*," Sundor said, "when a man attacks you?"

"*You're* not attacking me. You're *teaching* me." Elizabeth wiped mucus from her nose; she blinked tears from her eyes. "Your point is taken. Believe me."

Sándor looked away. His eyes softened. His mouth quivered. A flash of shame? He offered her a hand, but Elizabeth climbed to her feet and dusted off her trousers.

"What's next?" she said.

"Water," said Sándor.

Elizabeth stiffened. It took everything in her power not to respond to that word. She had never played poker, had never gambled, never had reason to lie. For years, Elizabeth had been abuzz with nervous habits; chewing pencils, chewing cuticles, tapping her foot, scratching at her knees. Her fidgets always drove her mother mad. But now she must act natural. She must be herself, and nothing else. But what *was* "herself"?

Sándor marched to the sink. Elizabeth watched, feeling like an imposter in her own body. The pain was receding now. Maybe Sándor hadn't yanked her hair as hard as she thought; or maybe she was tougher now, hardened, getting used to all of this physicality. She watched her big toe curl over its smaller neighbor, pressing into the carpet. Another anxious habit, something she'd never noticed she did.

Sándor drank greedily. Water splashed down his cheeks. It dampened his already sweat-stained shirt. He set down on the stump and exhaled loudly, like a castaway saved from drowning.

Sándor sauntered toward her, palms pressed into his hips. He studied the ground contemplatively.

"Perhaps you *have* done what I asked you," Sandor murmured. "Yesterday, I told you to *surprise* me. And now, I see you have. I have never met a student—man or woman— who would suffer in this way. Not when escape is so simple.

Let me ask—why did you not strike? Why did you not take a chance? Were you afraid to hurt me?"

"No," Elizabeth retorted. "I was afraid to be a coward."

She avoided his gaze, but she felt the halo of admiration. She had said something right. She had *impressed* him. And perhaps it meant the world to her—but she didn't want it. Not yet.

"Anyway," Elizabeth went on, "I take my homework seriously. And *that* was not the surprise."

Sándor smiled. It was the weary smile of a man who didn't know what he was smiling about. His feet stepped back on the carpet. "Now, we will practice tripping. This is very useful for a shorter fighter. A taller opponent does not have..."

Sándor paused. He narrowed his eyes.

He shook his head quickly. His cheeks waggled.

"They have a higher center of gravity," Elizabeth finished. "It's easier for them to fall over."

"That is... correct," Sándor replied.

But he sounded distant. Distracted. He advanced, but each footfall looked clumsy. As if testing the ground before he stepped.

"So, something like *this*..."

Elizabeth sprang, drawing her leg behind Sándor's. She pushed her hand against his chest, and he tumbled backward. His body flopped against the rug. He lay there, eyes aslant with confusion. A long, hollow breath puffed out of him. His fingers curled for a few seconds, then went limp.

Elizabeth surveyed the crumpled body, her face hard with scientific scrutiny. She crouched beside him, then held a hand over his face. She was relieved to feel the slow exhale.

"What you're feeling," she said, "is the venom of a puffer fish."

Sándor's eyes widened—the only sign of control over his immobile body.

"I was surprised to find it at the local apothecary," continued Elizabeth. "A very low dose, mind you, but enough to paralyze you. You'll have to stay like this for a few hours, I'm afraid. But you won't feel pain, and you'll certainly live. I may not be a doctor, but I know my way around a pharmacy. And by now you've probably figured out—I poured it into your pitcher while you weren't looking." She sniffed. "You asked for a surprise. There you have it."

Elizabeth reached into her satchel and drew a small glass vial. The same vial she had emptied into Sándor's water pitcher. She turned the glass vessel around in her fingers, watching the residue ooze from one end to the other. "Outsmarting my enemies is something I think I'm going to like."

Elizabeth was about to stand up. She was about to walk out. She had finished her scene, and now it was time for the curtain. But she couldn't help herself. She couldn't *stop*. She leaned down, placing a hand on Sándor's chest. She gazed deep into his hazel eyes—the color of rusted copper, two green universes gazing back at her. No longer afraid—but intent, fascinated. Defenseless.

Elizabeth's fingers traced his pencil mustache. She outlined the profile of his face. And then her head tipped, and their lips met. An awkward contact, for Sándor could not change the shape of his mouth. Their flesh was dry and chapped. Their breath was stale. Yet Elizabeth's heart throbbed in her temples. Euphoria surged through her. She relished this kiss—her first kiss—an act she'd never dared to dream of.

Slowly, Elizabeth lifted herself to her feet. She stuffed her legs back into her boots, and she returned the satchel to her shoulders. Flushed, cotton-mouthed, Elizabeth stood tall. She said, "Now, if you'll excuse me, I think I'll get a haircut."

❖

The building looked like an ordinary house, wedged between similar houses, and there was no sign above the transom. Elizabeth might never have known what went on inside, had she not passed the open door so many times. Heading into town, she saw young women disappear through the entryway; coming back, she saw the same young women emerge, their hair trimmed, gussied up.

Elizabeth liked what she saw, especially among the younger girls, who punctuated their dark curls with colorful ribbons and kerchiefs. Elizabeth could only admire the elegance of Spanish women, the bright hues and swishing pleats of their garments. Elizabeth thought morosely of the earthy tones back home, the gray suits and muted dresses that no amount of ornament could bring to life. Here, a young woman could tuck a rose behind her ear, wrap a scarf around her tresses and let the silken tendrils dangle. White blouses and paisley shawls complimented those shining black locks.

Elizabeth waltzed through the door, where she found a trio of women sitting in chairs. She said, in Spanish so breezy that she surprised herself, "*Me encantaría tener un corte de pelo, por favor.*"

One of the women nodded. She ushered Elizabeth through the house, to another door. Together, they entered a courtyard, situated in the middle of the building, shaded from the mid-afternoon sun.

Elizabeth sank into a chair, and a sheet was tied around her neck. The woman was plump and gray, and crow's feet emanated from her eyes. But when Elizabeth drew a folded piece of paper from her bag, the woman lit up. She smiled at the glossy scrap—a photograph, torn from a magazine, depicting a Hollywood starlet. The model was young, her skin papery smooth. Her hand was pressed coquettishly against her jaw. She looked upward, as if getting a good view of the moon. It was a standard glamour shot, typical of famous beauties, except for one thing: Her hair was cut into a bob. A single sheet of hair curved down from her head, hiding her ears, cutting diagonally toward her chin. The strands tapered into a sharp point. Bangs swooshed over her forehead. The look was topped with a bona fide beret.

Somewhere, Elizabeth had seen this style before. On the ship, perhaps, during her long passage across the Atlantic. On a platform, waiting for a train. Walking down the street, Elizabeth may have spied a *modern woman*, her hair flamboyantly short. And when she'd found this photograph, spotted by accident in to discarded magazine, it took her breath away. She studied this shimmery image—the woman she had always imagined herself to be. Not the matron in her picture hat; not the corseted ingénue; not the pale wife sipping tea; not the yards of fabric piled over shoulders and bust. Instead, something simple, untethered, *new*.

The shears came out, and they snipped. Tufts of hair fell away, tickling her skin, collecting at her feet. The hairdresser smiled a little wider with every cut, until she was giggling. Elizabeth doubted the woman had ever shaped hair like this before. Yet she cleared away the superfluous inches, straightened lines. At last, she set down her shears, clapped her hands together, and grabbed a hand mirror.

Elizabeth barely recognized herself. The crescents of hair fell around her cheeks like silken drapes. The texture of her face was creamy and alive, as if she'd stepped into a spotlight. Elizabeth had seen her reflection thousands of times before, in mirrors and shop windows, in pools of water and in polished metal. But she had never really *looked* at herself before. For the first time, she felt like a physical presence in the world, as real and profound as the pyramids.

"*Señora*," whispered Elizabeth. "*Gracias. Mil gracias.*"

"*Señorita*," replied the woman, "*con gusto. Usted es linda.*"

❖

As Elizabeth approached the gate, she wondered what would happen next. What are you supposed to say to a man once you've poisoned him?

The sky was overcast, and the crickets buzzed. She tied her horse in the shade, then nimbly rounded the familiar stone wall. She forced herself to breathe, though that simple act felt unnatural. Like all cautious gamblers, she had considered the worst—Sándor would exert his fury, berate her, report back to Dr. O'Malley. She would be exiled, excommunicated, stripped of all praise and encouragement. Or was there something worse in store?

Yes, she had done what Sándor asked. But she'd gone *further*. The surprise, the humiliation—it was more than most men could imagine. She must brace herself for anything.

She spotted Sándor, perched on his stump. She felt a flood of relief.

Sándor was wearing different clothes—a variation on his usual costume. His hair was slicked back, and his skin was freshly bathed. He had even shaved; his mustache was pronounced against razor-burned cheeks. At some point, he had risen from his paralyzed state. He had crawled, then walked, back to his stead. Not until this moment had Elizabeth truly considered the gravity of her deception; she had never administered a poison in her life. A slight mismeasure could have killed the man. Was this unfair? As fierce as his training could be, Sándor had never threatened her life. What harm she had suffered was cosmetic. She had turned the tables, upped the ante. She had toyed with his mortality. The poison was infinitely more than he had bargained for, and she knew it, and she had no defense. Not really.

Sándor was as statuesque as ever, his face inscrutable. His body did not shift. His eyes did not move. As if he had waited, immobile, for her arrival. His knees were bent, his boots rooted in the earth. His gloved hands were clasped, and he rested against his forearms.

Never had Elizabeth tried so hard to read a man's mind. To open up his thoughts and decide what he was thinking. The rugs were gone; the weapons were put away, covered in their blankets. Whatever happened next, they would be unarmed.

No words came to mind. None of her spitfire quips. No pleasantries, no jests. But neither did they come from him.

The light breeze sloshed in her ears. Thoughtlessly, she raised her hand to her hair and pushed it back, a gesture that was new to her. She suddenly remembered her metamorphosis; she was different, now. One day later, and she had emerged another woman. What did he see, now? A reckless brat? A rebellious naïf? Or still just a girl, a medical school dropout who couldn't even aim a gun?

His expression changed. His cheeks drizzled downward, like sand through an hourglass. Irises and eyebrows synchronized into a portrait of confusion. Emotion after emotion rippled through his face.

All at once, Elizabeth *knew*—it wasn't her prank with the poison. It wasn't the hours he'd spent prone on the ground. Not the haircut or the ineffable silence. The words they had exchanged had nothing to do with this moment. It was the other thing she had done. *The kiss.* That primal, gentle act.

Elizabeth felt herself sway. A jubilant, seasick feeling. Somehow, she knew that Sándor would stand up. She knew that he would charge at her. She knew she would raise her hands—not to swat him away, but to receive him. She could feel his hands before they enveloped her. She knew their lips would meet—the same sensation as before, but amplified, overwhelming. And then it went on—a kiss that surpassed the limits of her imagination. They smothered each other in kisses, caresses. Fingers sank into flesh. Her body hummed. They seemed to levitate, two aerialists entwined in the empty air.

Everything about this was right. It was the purest moment she had ever known. If she died tomorrow, at least she'd had this—the only thing that had ever truly mattered.

❖

Dazed, Elizabeth looked around.

Sándor lived inside the windmill. The ground floor was rustically renovated, and his quarters were improbably well furnished. Packing crates had been repurposed as chests and end tables. Ornamental textiles were draped over the splintery wood surfaces, each topped with pewter candelabras.

Elizabeth saw jugs and household nicknacks. Abstract tapestries clothed the whitewashed walls, half-hiding patches of raw brick, and shelves were bolted to masonry.

Afternoon light shot through the small, square windows. Smoke made mystical shapes in its golden rays. Elizabeth looked up, into the vaulted ceiling, where beams crisscrossed, ever higher, into the upper echelons of the windmill's trunk. Far above them, birds nested on the dormant gears, and cobwebs danced on the updrafts.

Naked beneath the sheets, Elizabeth wallowed in her bliss. She stretched luxuriantly across the plush mattress; her hair was frazzled, sticking crudely to her sweat-stained skin. She couldn't imagine moving; to crook a single toe was beyond her means. Her body was warm and limp, as if she had stepped out of a sauna and collapsed here, too pacified to go on.

Sándor was propped against the ornate headboard, a Turkish cigarette in his fingers, his arm resting on a bent knee. His other arm lay atop hers, his fingers caressing her knuckles. His body was dense with muscle and earth-colored hair. He didn't look like a sideshow strongman, as Elizabeth had secretly imagined his unclothed frame; instead, he had the physique of a laborer, practically sculpted by everyday use.

And what did *he* see—the only man ever to perceive Elizabeth in her totality? Until today, she had never really grasped what men desired in women. Not really. But now she understood—in the choreography of his movements; the focus of his hands; the way he'd traced her shape like a potter at his wheel. Sándor *knew* women, she realized, and he had ravished her practiced ease. For three years, Elizabeth had studied a thousand anatomical drawings, dissected cadavers, committed Latin words to memory. But somehow she had never felt at home in her skin. Now, in a few panting hours, she'd been schooled in the possibilities of her own form. She was not merely alive, but living.

"So," Elizabeth croaked. "What do we do now?"

The words surprised her. They hadn't spoken since the courtyard, communicating only in the language of seduction. How had she mustered such a stoic sentence? She didn't want to ruin this moment. She couldn't bear the notion of reality—this dream caving in—then back to the minutiae of regular life. Even the thrill of her journey, of existing in another world, of courting a secret society, was dwarfed by these blossoming sensations. Why did she have to speak? Why couldn't this feeling go on, a never-ending cycle of passion, exploration, zeniths of pleasure?

Through curls of smoke, Sándor said, "Things are different, now."

Elizabeth swallowed. "You can say that again."

Sándor stared straight ahead. And then, with an impish grin, he repeated, "Things are different now."

Elizabeth turned her head towards him. "No, it's just an express—"

But it was too late. Sándor was already chuckling. He knew. *Of course* he knew. His English was immaculate. He was joking. Again, Elizabeth felt a desperate relief, because he was laughing, and now *she* was laughing, too. For all her snide remarks, Elizabeth rarely laughed aloud. But now they were cackling like fools, because they *were* fools, reckless and ridiculous, lying in a bed together, shell-shocked with afterglow. No one knew, not a single soul in the world, the synchronicity of their joy.

The cigarette vanished, and Sándor descended to her side. He placed a hand in the middle of her chest, pressing against her heart. He surveyed her; his impossible eyes moved across her face like a spotlight.

"I ought to do something with my day," said Elizabeth. She touched his lips, then slid a finger across the bristles of his mustache. "Or else I'll convince myself that this is all there is."

Sándor blinked in slow motion. "Yes," he said. Then he rolled forward, his lips claiming hers. "But not quite yet."

❖

Elizabeth was just about to turn down her oil lamp when she heard a creak in the corridor. Her ears perked at the sound, and she set her pen on the desk. Instinctively, she slipped off her shoes and rose to her feet. Elizabeth tiptoed slowly across the room, wary of the floorboards that might betray her movement.

Another creak. She heard the squeal of old wood and the scuff of a heel. The direction was unmistakable; there was someone standing directly in front of her door.

As she moved past the bed, Elizabeth plucked the pistol from her bundled sheets and cocked it. The click, which sounded so dull in an open field, resounded in this silent little room.

In place of a handle, Elizabeth's skeleton key protruded from the lock. She reached the door and pinched the round head between her fingers. She held the gun in her other hand, leveling it against her stomach. A stream of breath escaped her nostrils, and then—she turned the key and threw open the door.

The dark figure recoiled. He wore a tweed jacket and spectacles. His hand was raised, clearly about to knock.

"*Jumping Jehosaphat!*" he cried.

"Professor O'Malley?" Elizabeth yelped. "What—what are you doing here?"

Dr. O'Malley pressed a hand against his chest, as if holding his heart in place. He adjusted his lenses and said coolly, "Well—Elizabeth—I had thought to invite you out for a drink."

"You *frightened* me!" Elizabeth exclaimed.

"The feeling's mutual." He nodded toward the pistol. "Truth be told, I'm still a bit anxious."

"Ah," said Elizabeth. She smirked and tossed the weapon back onto her mattress. "Don't be, the way I've been shooting." She shrugged. "A drink, you say?"

Dr. O'Malley smirked. "If you're not engaged."

"Professor," said Elizabeth, grinning. "I'm all yours."

❖

They walked down an empty street. Lamps glowed within each skinny house. Elizabeth spotted families within, seated around tables, eating their late-evening suppers. The whole town had retreated indoors, and Elizabeth and Dr. O'Malley had the outside to themselves. The intersections drew out, until all the streets seemed to flow into a single dirt road. Buildings were replaced with dark trees. The sky was open, spangled with stars, and a three-quarter moon poured light over their route. The air was cool, and the insects played their orchestra in the glade.

"This way," said Dr. O'Malley, diverging from the road.

Elizabeth paused, watching him disappear into black bushes. "Professor, I'd follow you anywhere, but…"

"Short-cut!" called Dr. O'Malley, with surprising distance.

Elizabeth picked up her pace. She stumbled over roots, then wrestled her skirts from unseen branches; but just as she was about to ask what kind of tavern could be stranded among the brambles, the land opened up. The dark shrubbery spread out, and Elizabeth saw dark rectangles in the grass. They leaned one way and another, like tired laborers.

"Your shortcut is a *cemetery?*"

Dr. O'Malley chuckled. "I suppose I should have warned you not to whistle," he said.

A match flared. Dr. O'Malley was crouching now, the hem of his field jacket curling around his bent legs. He leaned into a stone, and the tiny flame danced before the etched calligraphy. Nearby monuments, barely visible in the glow, looked old and mottled, but this granite slab was fresher; time had not yet softened the clean carving.

Dr. O'Malley fiddled with his spectacles. "Do me a favor," he said, "and read that inscription for me, would you?"

Elizabeth bent toward the stone. She read aloud, "En Paz Descanse—El Conde de Veszkovár, 1860 – 1895." She grimaced. "Should that mean something?"

"Everything in a graveyard means something to *someone,*" murmured Dr. O'Malley, straightening. He blew out the matchstick and flicked it into the renewed darkness. "But enough of that. Shall we?"

❖

There were wagons. Six in all, parked in a semicircle around a bonfire. Their wooden frames were painted in an array of faded pastels, which flickered before the flames. Men and women were crouched on the ground, holding each other in languid amorousness. Others sat alone, gazing at the fire. They spoke in low mumbles, their dialogue interrupted by the slosh of liquid from a bottle. A toddler in a ragged loincloth roamed among the bodies, caught and released by various hands, eliciting the occasional chuckle. Many of the women wore bandanas over their long hair; some men wore the floppy hats of alpinists. The scent of burning logs barely concealed the smell of their bodies. Most of them were barefoot, their heels and toes blackened.

Dr. O'Malley and Elizabeth stepped into the light, and a pair of men sprang to their feet. Upright, they looked haggard and thin. Their faces were dark and gaunt, and curled hair sprouted erratically from their faces.

The professor spoke. His cadence was the same as ever, that soothing lilt, but the language wasn't English. Elizabeth tilted her head toward the spoken greeting, trying to discern words, but it wasn't Spanish, either.

The men changed. Their faces blossomed with smiles. They jogged toward Dr. O'Malley, their footsteps clumsy, and they both threw their arms around him. They spoke, effusively, in the unknown tongue, tousling Dr. O'Malley's hair and smacking him on the shoulders. They gestured to a place by the fire and extended hands toward Elizabeth.

Dr. O'Malley spoke again, but the only word Elizabeth could discern was her own name. And just like that, she and Dr. O'Malley joined the circle of silhouetted figures, and the crowd came alive with conversation.

"Well, you stumped me," Elizabeth said. "What are they speaking?"

"That," Dr. O'Malley said reverently, "is Caló."

Elizabeth searched her memory. "Well, it's Greek to me."

"Nearly," chuckled Dr. O'Malley. "It's the language of the Romani. But you might know them better as gypsies."

Elizabeth gawked at her company. Were these really gypsies? The same gypsies that the townsfolk mocked and derided? The pickpockets and beggars that everyone had warned her against? Here, sitting in the open air with their children, chortling in the carefree way of adolescents? In town, people scornfully spat the word *Gitano*, but Elizabeth had rarely recognized the context, only the disgust.

"And these are—friends of yours?"

"More than that," Dr. O'Malley said. "And now it is time for you to know one of our *trade secrets*, if you will. All across Europe, and in places you never think of, the Romani are our most trusted informants."

Just then, a man fell sideways. He knocked into his companion like a bowling pin. The pair doubled over laughing. Together, they slurred some doggerel at the sky.

"You'll forgive me," murmured Elizabeth, "if your confidants don't inspire much—well, *confidence*."

"That's the trick, isn't it?" said Dr. O'Malley. He paused to tip a bottle, and liquid poured into his waiting gullet. He exhaled dramatically, then sucked air through his teeth. Elizabeth smelled his moonshine-infused breath, and it even stung her eyes.

"The Romani are everywhere," continued Dr. O'Malley. "Their network is vaster than anyone could map. They exist outside of any law or state. When a Roma sneezes in Transylvania, his brothers know of it in Portugal. They know every street and alley in Europe. And for centuries, they have been the Order's eyes and ears. Whatever we think we know, they know tenfold."

The bottle appeared before her. There was no label, no cork. A toxic odor rose from its neck. Yet Elizabeth didn't hesitate. She grabbed the bottle and slugged it back. The liquid hit her like a flash flood. She held the foul concoction in her mouth, then let it ooze down her esophagus. Her brain sparked. To her surprise, the sensation pleased her. This was not Dr. O'Malley's coffee spiked with scotch, but raw fermentation.

"Well done," said Dr. O'Malley. "You make a Paddy proud."

The slur sounded strange, coming from Dr. O'Malley, but Elizabeth smiled. His glasses were gone. He looked both younger and older than she remembered. One leg was balanced over the other, and he leaned into a bent arm. Unfettered by sobriety, Dr. O'Malley hinted of riskier days. She imagined his hardscrabble youth in the streets of Dublin, coarse words and spontaneous brawls. He had disguised that boyhood temperament so well, dressed himself up as a quiet academic. She could barely recall his presence in the classroom, the measured lessons that wafted from him like steam. How could a man so thoroughly reinvent himself? And how could he fall back so easily into the patterns of his youth?

Elizabeth took a humbler swig. "I saw something in town. A sword fight."

"Ah," said Dr. O'Malley. "Yes. A duel."

"You know?"

"That, Elizabeth, is why Sándor is here. It's the reason you have met him in Spain, and not in Budapest."

"I hope you won't leave it at that?"

Dr. O'Malley sighed cryptically. "The man you saw—the older man—is Don Iglesias Maritoña. He's a local nobleman. Although I use the term loosely."

"He lives here?"

"He does. In fact, he's lived here for quite some time." Dr. O'Malley sneered. "Three hundred years, to be precise."

Elizabeth started. "Three *hundred*..." She looked again into the fire, as if to find some explanation in the embers. "I hope that's hyperbole."

"It's not. It's quite literal. Sándor can explain better than I. He's quite obsessed with this particular case. But he has confirmed, to the best of our knowledge, that this man has been living in this town for all of three centuries."

"But—how?"

Dr. O'Malley nodded. He seemed to have asked the question many times himself. "That is precisely what Sándor intends to find out. The locals are tight-lipped, of course. Peasants usually are. But among that minority that still duel, Don Maritoña is something of a legend. Fencers from across Europe have challenged him. Or he challenges them—it's hard to say. This is the sort of Mediterranean bloodsport that has never interested me." He shrugged. "But he keeps on living. And *that* is the value of this case, as far as the Order is concerned. How does a man achieve such longevity? To know would be a boon for medical science. Or—" Dr. O'Malley darkened. "—a terrible weapon, in the wrong hands. As you know, this is the narrow road we tend to tread."

"Has he learned anything?"

"Not much. The man is a shut-in. Don Moritoña, I mean. Sándor—well, you've seen what kind of fellow he is."

Elizabeth bristled. For a moment, her intoxication lifted. "Have I?"

"*Haven't* you?" Dr. O'Malley turned to her. "I mean, not to speak ill of him. He's quite intelligent. A master of martial arts. We're lucky to count him among our own."

"But?"

Dr. O'Malley chuckled. His head lolled sideways. "It is my own bias. Nothing personal at all. I admire the man. I might even envy him, to tell the truth. But he *is* an aristocrat."

Elizabeth choked. "He's *what?*"

Dr. O'Malley sat up, suddenly self-conscious. "Well, a count, anyway."

"A *count?*"

"Didn't he tell you?"

"He's barely told me anything. A *count*, did you say?"

Dr. O'Malley snickered. "Well, for once, I admire his restraint. But yes, he had some sort of title. Back in Hungary. I dare not try to pronounce it. Some ancient dynasty. A lavish estate, I hear. And both his parents are gone, poor man. So it's all his. The castle. The tapestries. The hunting dogs. The usual lot of it."

Elizabeth was spellbound. All this time, Sándor had been a count. But then again, what did that mean? She felt, in that moment, more American than ever—a millionaire, she'd understand. Oil tycoons and senators and movie stars were part of her everyday lexicon. She could picture a newspaper mogul, slumped into an oversized chair, nursing a glass of port. But what did it mean to be a count, much less an Austro-Hungarian one? How had he grown up, on this fabled estate? Did it matter to him, this so-called title? Was it a point of pride? A burden? And why hadn't he told her, if everyone else knew?

A sound pierced the air. The unmistakable thrum of fingers over strings. Elizabeth looked toward the fire, and she saw a man rise into the smoke. A guitar was slung around his shoulders.

A woman appeared behind him. She was petite, muscular, with an aspect like an arrowhead. She stepped into the glow, and everyone rose to attention. Men called out; women clapped. The visitor raised her arms, and they twisted through the fire's sparks. Her long fingers pinched a pair of castanets.

The guitarist started to play. The melody was fast, spirited. He leaned into his instrument, as if kowtowing to the woman beside him. She, in turn, rearranged herself, articulating her arms like vines. The castanets clicked violently in her grasp. Her feet stomped the hard earth. Elizabeth craned her neck; the woman had long legs, and she wore unpainted wooden shoes. She pulled at the hem of her frilled skirt, and it swished from side to side, a hypnotizing flourish.

The man sang. The notes poured from him, rich and staccato. He ululated the untranslatable words. The woman danced; her head butted the air; her long hair slashed around her mournful face. She pounded and clacked, her legs flexing beneath the satin gown.

Elizabeth watched. And as she did, action and thought overlapped into one, a single fluid feeling. She slipped into memory—of that morning, the throes of passion—and the liquor's warmth imposed new meaning on her nerves. She felt so blessedly far away from anything familiar, so captured by this moment; the flamenco; the impossible cast of characters; the groundswell of esoteric knowledge. Who was she, to deserve such company, such ever-spreading veins of kinship and secrecy?

"How are you faring?" murmured Dr. O'Malley.

"Me?" said Elizabeth, gesturing for the bottle. "I'm the happiest girl on earth."

❖

Elizabeth woke to the drumbeat of her own head. She rolled from the bed, crawled to her medicine bag, and drew a toothbrush into the dim light. The curtains were mercifully pulled, yet she struggled to find her tooth powder. Soon her mouth was full of froth, and she was relieved to taste baking soda and peroxide, which scrubbed away the breath of the previous night.

She fought the urge to primp. Yes, she would see Sándor, and this reunion thrilled her down to her toes. But she already felt the late-morning heat, and he would wonder why she was so late. For that matter, what *would* happen now? How were they expected to resume? One morning ago, the future had seemed so distant. She hadn't thought much about the dawn, or how their next sparring session would transpire. What should she expect in the wake of—well, this recent turn of events?

Elizabeth pulled on her jodhpurs and blouse. It was the bare minimum, and she envied slovenly men who dressed in such uncomplicated ways. She threw her satchel over her shoulder, filled a bottle with water, and opened the door.

And there was Dr. O'Malley.

He leaned casually against the plaster wall, hands tucked primly into the pockets of his pinstripe vest. His hair was washed and brushed back, and his pointed chin was smoothly shaved. Even the round lenses of his spectacles looked polished. He pulled out his pocket watch, noted the time, and grinned. "Top of the morning to you," he said. "Shall we?"

"I… uh… I mean…"

Nausea welled up inside her. How had Dr. O'Malley groomed himself so completely? Was this even the same man—the reckless bohemian of the previous night? She saw the cloth bindle thrown over his shoulder, the kind carried by mountaineers. Had she forgotten some appointment, in the haze of inebriation?

She took a breath. "Where?"

"To see Sándor, of course," Dr. O'Malley said. "Not to worry. I brought my own horse."

That grin. There was something strange about it. Forced. Theatrical. Only now did Elizabeth realize how kind, how caring, the man had always seemed. This was something else. Another emotion. Her skin prickled. A chill ran through her. *What does he know?* she thought, suppressing panic. *Could Sándor have told him? Was this all a test? To see whether I could resist? Was I supposed to—to have feelings for him? Have I done something wrong? Or is this something else entirely?*

"Of course," Elizabeth said. "Checking in on the troops, I assume?"

"Yes," said Dr. O'Malley, pointedly. "Couldn't have phrased it better myself."

❖

Elizabeth couldn't remember a longer passage in her life. The horses ambled abreast, their shoes clicking against the ground. She swigged from her water, feeling greasy and morose. The good cheer had dried up with the punishing sun. Sloppy clouds mingled above, but not thickly enough to promise rain. Crickets shrieked all around them. She wondered if this was what condemned men felt like, on their march to the gallows.

They reached the windmill, and Elizabeth thirsted for the narrow shadows that circumscribed the walls. They dismounted, then guided their horses through the vacant gateway. She could barely force a breath as Sándor came into view.

One of the tables stood at the edge of the field, its surface cleared. Sándor sat atop, hands perched on knees. He was nearly as unkempt as Elizabeth, the sweat already bleeding through his shirt. His expression was even, but Elizabeth could detect traces of unease. He couldn't prevent the knitting of his brows, the defensive angle of his chin.

"Professor," he proclaimed. "You must forgive my appearance. I was not expecting you."

"Not at all," said Dr. O'Malley, moving toward one of the roof posts. He tied the reins expertly and patted the horse's snout. "I hope *you* will forgive the intrusion."

Sándor smacked his hands, then rubbed them together. They made a chalky sound that Elizabeth could hear from thirty paces. Only then did she realize that she had stopped. She was stock-still, waiting for the men to make their moves.

"Well, then," said Sándor. "To what do I owe the pleasure? You wish to assess our progress? You would like to see a demonstration?"

Dr. O'Malley's grin was fiercer than ever. "No," he said. "In fact, I have come for another reason entirely. And I must apologize to Miss Crowne, for even asking her here. But—I require a witness."

Elizabeth had never fainted, but she could have just then. Witness to what? Why this sudden change in temperament? What could they possibly discuss in private that she would need to know about? If not their—their *transgression*—what else could the professor want?

"I've been making inquiries," said Dr. O'Malley. "You might call it a peer review. About this nobleman of yours. The one you insisted that you should investigate."

"Ah," said Sándor. "The swordsman."

"Yes," said Dr. O'Malley. "This Don Moritoña. After all, he is reason we're here, and not in Austro-Hungary, where our members have always trained."

Sándor shrugged. "It is closer to England, at any rate. Not as far for Elizabeth to travel, yes?"

"And yet," pressed Dr. O'Malley, "I dare say, we've heard very little. Not that I'm surprised. You cannot waltz into the man's chateau and expect him to reveal the source of his long life."

Sándor sniffed. "Such men are tricky, yes?"

"Of course." Dr. O'Malley kicked at the dirt. "But not long ago, I started to wonder—why should *you* be interested in such a man? A swordsman, yes, like you. An aristocrat, like you. And a duelist." Dr. O'Malley removed his spectacles. "A duelist, like *your father*. Who, as Elizabeth can confirm, is buried in the cemetery not five miles from where we stand."

"I…" Elizabeth stammered. "What… what do you mean?"

"*En paz descanse*," recited Dr. O'Malley. "Isn't that what the headstone read?"

"Well—yes, but…"

"El Conde de Veszkovár," the professor continued. "The Count of Veszkovár, who left this earth in 1890. Thirty-five when he passed, poor man. And you—Sándor—only ten years old, were you not?"

Sándor darkened. His body turned to rock. Yet he didn't flinch. The same militant calm prevailed. "You are wrong," he said. "He *was* buried in this place. But my family exhumed his body—and secreted him to Hungary, to sleep among his ancestors. Only the stone remains."

Dr. O'Malley bobbed his head—the same way he considered a point in the classroom. His voice turned quiet. "I must confess, Sándor, I don't know what it means to love a father. To revere a man you do not fear. Or even to know such a man well. I don't know much, but I know our boyhoods were well different."

Sándor's head whipped sideways. As if he'd been slapped. He mouthed something.

"He was challenged, wasn't he?" said Dr. O'Malley. "Some twenty-three years past. Called out to a duel. Against this Don Maritoña. He could not refuse, could? Honor forbade him to decline. And he went, did he not? Came to this very village. Drew swords against Don Moritoña. And it was here, in town square of Santo Demetrio, that he met his end."

Sándor vaulted from the table. He paced, his body moving ferally over the dead grass.

"You're not here to *investigate* a thing," Dr. O'Malley declared, his voice rising. "You're here to challenge the bastard yourself. You're here for *revenge*."

Everything inside Elizabeth drained away. Poured out of her. She was empty, without words or sensation. She felt so stupid—standing dumbly, next to her borrowed horse, oblivious.

Sándor stomped in circles, a wounded animal.

Revenge. All this time, he'd hidden this burden, this secret motive. A thing that had nothing to do with her, or Spain, or anything else. This count. This tortured orphan. A stranger. Yesterday, she had presumed to read his soul. Now? Who *was* he?

And what was *she* to him? How could she, a middling apprentice, ever measure against the tempest of his past?

Sándor stopped. He drew himself up. He stared maliciously at Dr. O'Malley. "And what of it?"

"Don't," commanded the professor. "Whatever you plan to do—and I have a keen idea what it is—do *not* do this thing. I implore you. The differences we've had—you and I—forget them, man. If you kill him, it will change nothing. And if you die…"

Elizabeth gasped. Not a gasp, but an upheaval. A sputter. A spasm. Her eyes demanded tears.

But Sándor didn't seem to see her at all. He only glared at his accuser.

"If I die," he growled, "then I have still done my duty."

Duty. Duels. Death. Nothing to do with her. An old feud. Vengeance. Violence. The same as she had seen in the plaza. She flashed to that moment, the sword bobbing in the young man's chest. The blood.

Elizabeth whirled away. The reins fell from her grasp. She ran. The gate flashed past her. She found the road, but she ran diagonally through the wild grasses. All she could hear were her own choking sobs. The hysteria of a slighted girl. A tricked child. A fool. She ran, gasping, down the long hill, toward those abysmal rooftops, toward that mocking steeple. The bell began to clang. The hour was changing. An hour closer to Sándor's death. An hour farther from her family, from her girlhood, from everything familiar. The bell tolled and tolled, until all she could feel was the heat and the crunching earth and the end of the world as she'd known it.

❖

Elizabeth stared at her baggage. One large suitcase, strapped shut. All her worldly possessions. The clothes, the knickknacks, the notebooks and toiletries, stuffed tightly into a single package of fabric and leather. She had always traveled light, and taken pride in this habit. Yet now it seemed so unremarkable. A whole material existence, lying inanimate on her desk.

She fondled the train ticket in her fingers. A single piece of paper, which would extricate her from this place. She could barely remember the walk to the station, the ticket window, or the graying man in the peaked cap who asked her destination. Entranced, she had forked over the cash, then meandered back to the hotel. She'd packed without feeling; by now, arranging her things was as automatic as eating. From here, Barcelona. A spontaneous decision. But from there, who knew? Her final stop was Pittsburgh, of course, but she had little idea how. She couldn't imagine the tracks that ran beyond that first terminal. She hadn't imagined the steamer that awaited her. She still had enough cash, wadded within her suitcase, to book her passage, as long as she scrimped on meals and stayed in only the meagerest lodgings. A long slog lay ahead, and all along the way she'd have to carry this paltry, shattered heart.

The sun burned crimson through the curtains. She yearned for the promise of night. She could sleep away this day, the pain in her head, the failure that everything had led to. Then what? She didn't care. Only to wander through space, through crowds, and pare away her humiliation.

The door fell open.

She'd forgotten to lock it. There, in the darkness of the hallway, stood Dr. O'Malley. His legs were spread, his hands balled at his waist. Confident as ever. He looked at her with knowing eyes.

Elizabeth said nothing. But she couldn't help herself. Her practiced sneer melted before the professor. She rose from the bed. She flew across the room, threw her arms around Dr. O'Malley, and spewed her sobs into his shoulder. For the first time, she felt his wiry frame; she smelled the pipe smoke embedded in his clothes, and she wished, more than ever, that *this* was her father, hand wrapped around her hair, his other hand pressing into her back.

"There, there," he cooed. "Don't think I blame you a bit."

"*Why?*" she choked into her chest. "*Why would he?*"

They stood there for a long time, cradled in the darkness of the corridor.

Too soon, Dr. O'Malley released her. "Perhaps a gift will make you feel better."

At first Elizabeth couldn't see the object through her soggy eyes. But then it materialized—a tiny bauble, gray as pewter, pinched between his thumb and index finger. A ring. Tiny, roughly cast. And there, clearly embossed, the insignia of the Order of Seshat.

"Oh, Lord," sniffled Elizabeth. "It's even my color."

Dr. O'Malley grinned. "This ring is five generations old. I can't begin to reckon the miles it's traveled." He took Elizabeth's hands, then slid the heavy circle onto her finger. "A token of our fellowship. May you be recognized by any member, anywhere in the world."

Elizabeth sniffed. "Or in Pittsburgh, at any rate."

Dr. O'Malley cocked his head. "Eventually," he said.

"Eventually?"

"Well, it's time to discuss your stipend."

"My—what?"

Dr. O'Malley's grin turned impish. "A bank account has been issued in your name."

"In *my* name?"

"Indeed. And from this day forth, you shall be wired a sum of two hundred United States dollars, every month, for the remainder of your life."

Elizabeth blanched. She twisted the ring around her finger. "Two *hundred?* Every *month?*"

"Barring inflation, of course," Dr. O'Malley added, barely containing his satisfaction.

"But—that's nearly as much as my *father* makes."

"I imagine so. And for good reason. This stipend is to liberate you from lesser work. So that you may concentrate wholly on your investigations—wherever they may lead you. You need never concern yourself with the toil of supply and demand. You must focus only on your task—to explore the uncanny, and to report your findings back to us." Dr. O'Malley removed his glasses and began to clean them against his shirt cuff. "So, by all means, return to Pittsburgh. But until then, you are free. To go anywhere. To see anything. So if you want my opinion, take the scenic way back. For the world, Elizabeth, is yours."

If she took so much as a breath, Elizabeth feared this moment would expire, and she would awaken from the dream, back to the glum existence she'd always known. She couldn't believe that anything she'd ever done—ever *could* do—should merit such generosity. Yet here it was, the gift of a lifetime, sealed with a century-old trinket.

"Professor... I..."

"And *another* thing," Dr. O'Malley snapped. "I'll have no more of this *Professor O'Malley* business. For heaven's sakes, call me Colin."

Elizabeth guffawed. Her head swam. She patted him on the shoulder. "I... yes, all right—*Colin*."

"We're *colleagues* now," he said. "I am not your professor. Not your boss man. I am only here to guide you. To the best that I can. Because..." He squeezed her hand. "Because you have more than proved your mettle. And there's a great future ahead of you. Of that I'm certain."

He smiled again, then bowed his head. "Till we meet again." And with that, he walked away.

Stunned, flabbergasted, Elizabeth stood there, wishing she knew what to do with her frantic pulse. But then she thought of something—and she flew through the door.

"One last thing!" Elizabeth called down the hall. "What do I call myself?"

Dr. O'Malley—Colin—turned. "What's the matter with your given name?"

"No! I mean—how should I introduce myself? Is there a title I should use? Am a detective? An inspector? Some such thing?"

Colin was only a dark outline now, but she could see the man shrug. "Funny. No one's ever asked. What do you want to be called?"

Elizabeth spoke before she could think. "If we pursue the uncanny—is there such thing as an *uncannologist?*"

Colin sputtered. The opaque silhouette bent over with amusement. "Not that a know of."

"Then—I suppose I'll be the first."

Colin raised a finger to his forehead, saluted her, and turned down the staircase. The creek of his footsteps receded, until all she could hear was a wagon outside, and the caw of a bird, and children yelling far away. Now she was alone, free, freer than she had ever been in her life.

"Elizabeth Crowne," she said aloud. "Uncannologist."

❖

How did Sándor find her?

She had never been to the church in the middle of town. She had never ventured inside, never seen the rough marble pillars, nor the vaulted stone ceiling. Light sliced through the narrow windows, yet most of the choir was shrouded in cool darkness. Elizabeth sank into her pew, its wood smoothed and scratched from centuries of use. She leaned forward, pressing her head into cradled arms. She waited there for awhile, relishing the cool air, the dry isolation. Then she sat back— and there was Sándor.

Elizabeth should have been startled. She hadn't heard him sit down; his weight on the same bench didn't alert her to his presence. Yet somehow she *wasn't* surprised. The man was undetectable, when he felt like it. He had probably trailed her here, watched her from afar, sneaked through the door behind her. Elizabeth sighed through a veil of messy hair. There they were, in a church—of all places—together.

All around them, scattered penitents sat. The choir echoed with their whispered prayers. Elizabeth saw candles burning in the corner of her eye, the flickers of hope. She waited for Sándor to speak, knowing that he was waiting for her. In all her skeptical years, an old basilica was the last place Elizabeth expected to find herself seeking sanctuary. Yet here, in the Spanish *campo*, all the rules seemed to get rewritten.

"I don't know much about honor," Elizabeth muttered. "But I *do* know you're a fool to fight him—this Don Maritoña."

"Elizabeth—" tried Sándor.

"And I *also* know," she continued, "that there's nothing I can do to stop you. So whatever you have to say, say it. I'm not waiting around this podunk little town just to watch you die."

Sándor swallowed hard. The sound seemed to reverberate in the vast space. "If it was your father…"

"It *wasn't*," Elizabeth snapped. "*My* father is a physics professor who can never find his pocket square. It's apples and oranges. *He* didn't spend his life throwing down gauntlets, for heaven's sake. He's a gentle little man with gentle little hobbies. The most offensive thing he's ever done is drink too much sherry on Christmas Eve and make up limericks. If he so much as swung a fist, he'd probably break his own nose. So if you think I can imagine what it's like to lose my father to a godforsaken *sword fight*, you're sorely mistaken. That's a cross I doubt I'll ever have to bear." She paused, breathing hard, and brushed newly shorn hair from her eyes. "And I'm sorry *you* have to bear it. I am. It must be terrible."

"Then you understand," said Sándor. "Why I must do this."

"*No*," retorted Elizabeth. "I don't. And frankly, I never will. And if I thought begging would change your mind, I'd grovel at your feet—and I wouldn't stop until you dropped this whole sordid business. But that won't do any good. We both know that. So I'll spare us both the embarrassment."

Sándor turned to her, his arm resting on the back of the pew. "I can *win*. I can defeat him. Three centuries of death— they will end in a moment. Avenged forevermore."

"Maybe," Elizabeth said. "Or maybe you *won't* win, and you'll just be another headstone in that sad little graveyard. But know this, Sándor…"

Her voice cracked. She couldn't help it. The anger was giving way to another feeling—and the two emotions wrestled for control of her vocal chords.

"Know *this*," she said. "Either way—win or lose, live or die—*I will never forgive you.* Never in my life. And maybe I'm nothing to you. Why should I mean something, after so little time? But if I do—if I was ever more than just a fling—then you're *throwing it all away.* The second you pick up that sword is the second you decide never to see me again. So you can have your revenge. You can do your damnedest. *Or* you can have a shot at me. But you can't have both."

Sándor looked up, toward the ribbed ceiling. Ahead, the altar stood. A parade of biblical figures rose before them, a carved display of saints and heroes.

"I am a proud man," Sándor said slowly. "But I never presumed to deserve you."

Elizabeth clambered to her feet. "That's a very pretty thing to say," she spat. "I wish I had a pretty way of saying *go to Hell.*"

❖

In her saddest moments, Elizabeth had always felt comfort in a railroad platform.

All through her girlhood, she could escape an unpleasant day by climbing into a trolley car. At eighteen, when life seemed bleakest, her father drove her to the train station, and the locomotive chugged away, into the gray afternoon, toward Saint Luke's. When classes bogged her down, Elizabeth took the train home, celebrating Christmas in Pittsburgh. When that became insipid, and the gifts had been unwrapped, and the old rivalries surfaced with her sister, and her mother and father retreated to their separate rooms, the train was always there, ready to carry her away.

The Santo Demetrio station was small—little more than a cracked stone block topped with a rustic shelter. A couple of farmers sat on benches, draped in the shade, their straw hats pulled low. Some bags were piled nearby; a mangy hound sniffed the corners. There was nothing ceremonious about this departure. No farewell party. No one asking her destination. All those weeks, living in town, exploring its streets, coming so far, and now she was alone.

And yet, wasn't it better this way? To slip away, down the line, to another undiscovered place?

The train already stood before her, a sleeping giant. The ten passenger cars were sparsely peopled, judging from the windows. Figures lumbered past the dust-matted glass. Up ahead, the engine hissed and sputtered. A clerk stepped off, sweating in his cap and lapels, and idly examined the undercarriage. Elizabeth stood there, groping the handle of her suitcase, and gazed at nothing.

Barcelona, she thought. Hours and hours from now, she would be standing in that fabled seaside city. She would visit museums and wander the streets. Somehow, money would reach her, and she would begin her task. She felt a tinge of excitement. Barcelona, yes, but that was just a start. Where would she go? Not Pittsburgh—not yet. She could return whenever she wanted; and so much awaited her. Names rushed through her head—Paris. Rome. Berlin. All those capitals, with so many towns and villages in between. Castles and cathedrals. Haciendas and ancient cellars. Tombs, taverns, tall buildings, and endless rivers.

Yet why stop there? Now she was flipping through memorized maps, well-thumbed encyclopedias, the photographs she had pored over in her youth. Curled up on her bed with a copy of *National Geographic*, hadn't she dreamed of precisely this? Ottoman mosques? Egyptian pyramids? Jungles and deserts, mountains that disappeared into clouds, the vast expanses of the Earth? She flashed back to those stuffy classrooms, the white-out Berkshire winters, the mounds of half-read textbooks, and she snickered. What suckers they were, the young men in lab coats, falling asleep at their hutches. Even they, bright future physicians, couldn't hold a candle to the things she could do. Elizabeth felt weightless. She could do anything now. She was her own compass. How many girls—how many *anyone*—could claim such absolute freedom?

And then she heard it. The bells.

The same bells she had heard the other day. The bells that called all the people to Santo Demetrio to its central plaza. The same sonic preamble—to duels, death.

Her temples throbbed. She could still board the train. She could leave this place. She owed nothing to anyone. Couldn't she survive a little heartbreak? *Shouldn't* she? Get away? Forget this place ever existed? Remember her promise, to find the uncanny, to report back? To live the life that so few could? Shouldn't that life start now?

But then, all at once, she remembered the contents of her suitcase.

Freedom and desire collided in her brain, and her vision sparkled. Yes, she had agency. But she could also *stay*. She could finish the task; end the cycle; commandeer the madness once and for all. She had used force before, and she'd never regretted that fateful choice. She could act. She *must* act.

Elizabeth whirled around. She scampered across the platform, down the steps, and into the road. She ran. But she only ran a short distance before she heard the hum of an engine. Elizabeth turned, and there was a car, hobbling over the rocks and potholes. She waved her arms, frantic, and nearly threw herself at its fender. The car halted, and a bearded man leaned out. Her wore spectacles and a bowler hat.

"*Por favor!*" she cried. "*Deben llevarme al centro del pueblo!*"

She had never spoken such immaculate Spanish. The man's mouth was agape. He was stunned. But he couldn't deny her desperation. He simply nodded, and Elizabeth rounded the bumper, yanked open the door, and pointed ahead. The car rolled forward, toward the middle of Santo Demetrio, toward the sound of the clanging bells.

❖

The crowd was too thick to drive. The driver groped the steering wheel anxiously as bodies clustered all around. He looked helplessly at his passenger, as if to ask how far he should go.

Elizabeth couldn't wait. She dove from the car and into the fray, shrieking a "Gracias!" as she went. She barreled through the bodies, shoving passersby aside with the bulk of her suitcase. She climbed the hill, step by frantic step. Her ankle gave way, but she ignored the sprain. Faces finally turned, surprised at her presence, and the crowd began to part. Elizabeth climbed the final rise, sweat stinging her eyes. She tripped, but hands reached out to catch her. Murmurs and shouts lined her path; the noise swelled. Elizabeth pushed through the final throng, and then she was free—standing in the open air, that makeshift arena, where there was nothing but two men.

The fight had already begun. *More* than begun. They had already been fencing for some minutes. From what she could tell, the duel was nearly over.

Sándor lay on the ground, legs kicking at the dust. One hand clutched his sword; the other hand pressed against his face.

But not his whole face—his *eye*.

Blood dripped down his cheek. His forehead was creased with pain. His second eye was closed. He was out for the count. Within the minute, it would all be over.

Don Moritoña stood some paces away. Bigger than she remembered. A tiger in black clothing. His impassive face had changed; he was smiling. Joy. Demonic mirth. A joke that only he understood.

Elizabeth dropped the suitcase. She ripped it open. She yanked her pistol into the air. She raised it at Don Moritoña. She clutched the weapon in both hands, just as she'd been taught.

Yet the barrel shook. She slipped her finger into the ring, felt the crescent of its trigger. She watched the weapon rattle in her hand. The Mauser C96 expressed every fear she'd ever felt—every doubt, every second guess.

"*Atrás!*" she screamed. "*Atrás, hijo de puta!*"

Don Maritoña looked at her. His eyes turned calm. Mocking. He turned his sword sideways, point to the ground, as if pushing aside a curtain. His smile grew. His cheeks bulged. The look of a man who had betrayed death. The visage of careless evil.

Wordlessly, he advanced. Swift steps, gaining speed. The distance between them shrank. The sword rose. Elizabeth could see the point of it, aimed for her heart. He came, foot crossing foot, deft as a tightrope walker. His face tightened with concentration. This is was last thing a hundred men had ever seen—the furrows of his hatred, crowding out all else.

And then—another figure. In motion. Flying through the air.

Screams, high and shrill.

A sword, passing diagonally across her vision. Lashing out at Don Maritoña. Sliding through his neck. Piercing the other side. Ripping away, with a spatter of blood.

Sándor, heaving behind him.

The tercentennial swordsman froze in mid-air. He turned slightly, gobsmacked. He saw Sándor, his vanquisher. Don Maritoña patted his carotid artery. He touched the narrow hole. He sensed the maroon geyser that poured over his chest. He stepped sideways, woozy. The sword clattered over mortared stone. He nodded, acknowledging the truth of this moment—that now, after three centuries, his time had come.

He tumbled forward. Drew knees to chest. Held himself close, like a fetus in the womb, returning to oblivion.

❖

The hospital was too bright. The walls were whitewashed with sunlight. Elizabeth walked between the rows of beds, shielding her eyes with a hand.

Each mattress was occupied by a different kind of patient—a boy with skinned knees, a woman covered in bruises, an old man babbling to himself on the edge of the wooden frame. Nuns puttered about in their gray habits, carrying trays and fresh blankets. Only at the end did she find Sándor, stretched across his padding, sheets removed—a bandage stretched over half his face.

His good eye blinked at the sight of Elizabeth. He bent his elbows, trying to sit up, but he only winced. He turned his head away, looking myopically at the dusty corner.

Elizabeth carried her suitcase. The curve of her hair was carefully brushed; her linen dress was crisply laundered. Her most recent purchase—a woven fascinator with a plume of ribbons—tilted prettily to one side. She had primped for this moment, as much as she ever had.

Now they were here, together, in the whispery quiet of a hospital ward. Crossing town one last time, Elizabeth had wondered what they would say. Really, what *could* she say? Yet somehow, as Elizabeth looked at Sándor, lying here helplessly, his shame emboldened her. Smirking, Elizabeth said, "Well, this isn't the best you've ever looked in bed."

Sándor chuckled. He couldn't help himself. Still, he looked away, but the anguish faded. He lifted a hand to scratch his noble nose.

"I'm off," said Elizabeth, as casually as she could. "This is goodbye."

Sándor squeezed his one eye shut. It pained her to see it—such oracular beauty, reduced by half.

"It seems we've both gotten what we came for," she said.

Sándor exhaled. "I have learned," he said, "only recently, that the things we have come for are not always the things we find."

"And how."

Sándor turned toward her. His eye gleamed. "The deed is done. My obligation is met. Now, I will go home. And…" He swallowed. "I would be honored for you to come with me."

Elizabeth sighed. And in the length of this sigh, she dove deep into the recesses of her mind. Because she couldn't blame him, not really. Here was her prince, who did what princes did—sweep their maidens away to distant castles. Transform bookish girls from Pittsburgh into the dames of mansions. And maybe she could force herself to want that life. Maybe she could forgive him. Maybe she could trust him again—with her body, her safety, her heart—but not *this*. Tomorrows were a sacred thing, now more than ever. What use was a palace, a dashing paramour, a sprawling estate, and Lord knew what other excesses, if Elizabeth only exchanged one quiet room for another? And even if they worked together, lived together, journeyed together to the far corners of the Earth, would Sándor share his glory? Or would he just invite her along, a trusty woman at his side? Elizabeth sighed that thought away. She didn't want *his* glory. She was through with his traditions and heirlooms and feuds. Now, she needed her own.

"I think I've had my fill of honor," she said. "And I've already bought a ticket. So—this is where we part ways."

Sándor offered the slightest nod. "I will write to you. A letter every day."

Elizabeth frowned. "And where do you plan to send these letters?"

"To Pittsburgh, of course. To your home."

"Save the ink," said Elizabeth. "I don't plan to be there for a good long while."

"Well, then," said Sándor, summoning a smile. "You will have a great deal to read."

❖

Elizabeth walked down the hall. She picked up speed. She trotted into the stairwell, then skipped down the steps. She jogged through the vestibule, where orderlies eyeballed her with surprise. She dashed out the door, suitcase swinging at her side. She flew through the front door, into platinum sunlight.

On the train, she could hardly sit still. Her foot tapped the floor. She chewed her fingertip, gazed out the window, bit her lip, scratched her elbow. She needed this car to move, to pull out of the station and carry her away. She needed to see everything, do everything, meet everyone. She would go and go, consuming everything in her path, and no pitfall or dead end would stop her. *Brace yourself, world*, she thought. *I'm coming for you.*

When the torture finally ended, and the train began to chug away from Santo Demetrio, Elizabeth tore a blank page from her journal. She licked the tip of her fountain pen, looked squarely at the paper, and paused. She thought for a long time. The pen made tiny circles in the air. Outside, the hills rolled along. Towns and forests came and went. Shadows lengthened. The sun burned through the curtains.

Only then, when dusk was imminent, and the light was nearly too dim to write, did Elizabeth settle on something to say. It wasn't enough. It could never be enough. But she had a whole lifetime to elaborate. And that lifetime felt longer by the minute. She pressed the pen into paper.

Dear Abner,

It begins.

ACKNOWLEDGEMENTS

A great deal has happened in the past few years, most of it unexpected. When *The Mysterious Tongue of Dr. Vermilion* was published in 2016, the book existed in a vacuum. First, I must thank Don DiGiulio, the No Name Players, and The Arcade Theatre for helping me bring the first Elizabeth Crowne "live radio show" to the stage. This experiment helped prompt the podcast, and I owe limitless thanks to thousands of listeners; the stories are always fun to dream up, but it is your participation that makes them worth telling. Certain individuals and organizations have helped spread the name Elizabeth Crowne, including Richard Gibney, Paul Di Filippo, Megan O'Neill, Jodie Noel Vinson, and the whole crew at What Cheer Writer's Club. I am especially beholden to Kerry McKenna, Ryan Pradit, Alyssa Anderson, and Jessica Hatem for performing in the podcast and so dramatically enriching such a monkish experience. Special thanks go to Megan Schmit, whose keen editorial eye made this manuscript so very much more readable. And most of all, eternal love and thanks to Kylan and Leo, for all the adventure one could ask for.